VINTAGE

DATTAPAHARAM

V.J. JAMES writes in Malayalam. Born and brought up in Changanacherry, Kerala, he currently resides in Thiruvananthapuram. An engineer by profession, he worked at the Vikram Sarabhai Space Centre. The English translation of *Corashasthram*, titled *Chorashastra*, was shortlisted for the Atta Galatta-Bangalore Literature Festival Book Prize. The English translation of *Anti-Clock* was shortlisted for the JCB Prize for Literature 2021 and longlisted for PFC-VoW Book Award 2022.

MINISTHY S. is an IAS officer working in the Uttar Pradesh cadre. She translates between three languages: Malayalam, English and Hindi. She has translated four novels by V.J. James: *Anti-Clock*, which was shortlisted for the JCB Prize for Literature 2021, *Nireeswaran*, *Dattapaharam* and *The Book of Exodus*, all published by Penguin Random House India.

PRAISE FOR THE BOOK

'The search for a missing man turns into an exciting quest into the wellsprings of our being. V.J. James's *Dattapaharam* is a tantalizing modern fable that takes its place with the very best in contemporary Indian fiction'—**Paul Zacharia**

Dattapaharam
Call of the Forest

V.J. JAMES

Translated from the Malayalam by
MINISTHY S.

VINTAGE
An imprint of Penguin Random House

VINTAGE

Vintage is an imprint of the Penguin Random House group of companies
whose addresses can be found at global.penguinrandomhouse.com

Published by Penguin Random House India Pvt. Ltd
4th Floor, Capital Tower 1, MG Road,
Gurugram 122 002, Haryana, India

Penguin
Random House
India

First published as *Dattapaharam* by DC Books in 2005
Published in Vintage by Penguin Random House India 2023
This edition published in 2025

ISBN 9780143472391

Typeset in Berkeley by Manipal Technologies Limited, Manipal
Printed at Gopsons Papers Pvt. Ltd., Noida

www.penguin.co.in

100%
Paper from well-
managed forests
FSC® C191020

To all my dear friends
—V.J. James

To my brother, Hari
—Ministhy S.

'Life is not about the people who act true to your face.
It's about the people who remain true behind your back.'

CONTENTS

AUTHOR'S NOTE

WHEN THE SELF IS APPROPRIATED

On reading *Dattapaharam*, the response of one reader, who had been faithfully following the works of 'V.J. James the writer', was 'the book went over my head!' Another reader wrote, '*Dattapaharam* is a book which I hold close to my heart.' I prefer to accept both the reactions with equal love. Though I have published seven novels and nearly seventy short stories, if you were to ask me, I would reiterate that *Dattapaharam* offered me the greatest challenge as a writer. The reason would be that the state of existence unfurled in the novel is rare in the panorama of human experiences.

Comparatively, it is comfortable to write a philosophical book: you can state the facts in a straightforward manner. However, to effectively portray a unique vision of life via the intrigues of fiction is analogous to a dangerous trapeze act. If one is not exceptionally careful, it is easy to lose one's footing. And hence, extreme alertness was needed while writing

Dattapaharam. Of course, it is for the readers to decide how successful I have been in that endeavour.

Any human in this world understands hunger, thirst, pain and love because she/he has experienced it. Children can love but cannot lust; that state is beyond their comprehension. There are certain experiences unique to the President of America. For the Holy Pope, there are special experiences reserved exclusively for him. Some matters are cognizable only to the experts of space science or microbiology. In the same way, there are certain aspects of the world that can be experienced only by Freddie Robert—the protagonist of the novel—or those whose internal frames of mind are similar to his—an ineffable state where the self gets appropriated.

For some, it can 'go over the head'. For others, 'it can be close to the heart'. For such people, the novel might trigger a reverberation within. This book is meant for those who have undergone surreal experiences. Maybe there are a few. It could even be a single person! Even so, *Dattapaharam* is meant for him/her. There are many readers—like Lal Jose, the famous Malayalam film director—who, while caught in the thrill of their reading experience, called me and passionately shared their feelings. Those who love forests and nature will find it easy to merge with Freddie and comprehend him in his quintessence. Freddie exists where all the coverings get removed. I offer the same welcome to those who can mingle with Freddie and those who might look on in misapprehension.

Dattapaharam is the fourth book of mine—after *Anti-Clock*, *Nireeswaran* and *Chorashastra*—which Penguin Random House has published. For bringing it out in such an elegant manner, I express my heartfelt gratitude to the publishing house and its brilliant team members—especially Elizabeth Kuruvilla, Vineet Gill and Ahlawat Gunjan, who designed the book cover.

I express my thanks to Ministhy S., who ensured that the intrinsic beauty and spirit of the original work in Malayalam was not lost in translation.

The four years that I spent in the verdant environment, surrounded by hills, of Mar Athanasius College of Engineering at Kothamangalam helped me craft this book. There was a club called Sahitya, which encouraged students to get together on the last Thursday of every month to discuss their creative works. In my final year, I read out a story there, 'The Hymn of the Gang'; this transformed into *Dattapaharam* decades later. By that time, my views about life and the universe had undergone a sea change.

Almost twenty-five years later, I returned to the campus which had shaped me and retraced my paths in the surroundings described in *Dattapaharam*, undergoing an exultation which is yet to leave me. I felt Freddie Robert's presence then. The corridors emblazoned with his footprints, the shadow of the gulmohar, the hostel, the playground hewn off a hillock, the flowering erikku tree: nothing had changed. I can vouch that my experience, as I walked with my wife and children through the same spaces which I had explored with my friends years before, was a distinctive one. Freddie Robert, who had captivated many, held me in his thrall too. The same Freddie might converse with many in the intimate hours of reading. He might lead them to the wild forests, holding them by their hands.

A mother once wailed, 'Dear Krishna, do not venture into the wild forest!' One should step into wild experiences only with the temerity of having overcome that forewarning. Only then will it dawn on us that the one who forbids is the one who calls.

V.J. James

TRANSLATOR'S NOTE

Dattapaharam is the third book by V.J. James that I have been fortunate to translate. It is a deceptively simple novel, but as Leonardo da Vinci said, 'Simplicity is the ultimate sophistication.' One realized that truth while translating this power-packed little book.

Every book of James's has a different tenor and mood to it. If *Anti-Clock* has a black humour suffusing the whole script, *Nireeswaran* shimmers with philosophical insights. In *Dattapaharam*, it is the sense of surreal mystery that prevails across the narrative.

Since I was not familiar with the world of birds and forests, this translation required a lot of reading too. As I was desperately searching for the 'bird which supports the skies', aka *manamthangi kili*, to my delight, I found a reference to the *tithiri*, or the red-wattled lapwing (which is supposed to sleep on its back with its legs up) in the 'Aranya Kanda' of *Shri Ramcharitmanas*, which I was translating simultaneously! Now that was a herald of propitious beginnings.

The original novel has been loved by readers in Malayalam, and my hope and prayer is that the translation will also find a place in the hearts of many across the globe.

11 November 2022   Ministhy S.
Lucknow

The Valley News

Mysterious Man in Deep Forest

14 August: A mysterious forest dweller has been sighted by a team of environmental researchers who have been visiting the interiors of Pullothikkadu, twenty kilometres from the valley, to conduct the feasibility study for a dam. The stark-naked man was seen in an obscure and deep part of the forest uninhabited even by the tribal population. With his straggling long hair and beard, the primitive man resembled someone from beyond the Stone Age. Although the team searched long and hard for the man, who vanished into the deeper parts of the forest on sighting the researchers, their efforts were in vain. The search is continuing, as per reports.

Special update:

The office being closed today on account of Independence Day, there shall be no print edition tomorrow.

1

THE NEWS

On reading the news enclosed within the rectangular box in the newspaper, I sat dumbfounded. It had been eight months since we had lost Freddie Robert in the forest. Quickly emerging from the restraints of the rectangle, I dialled Sudhakaran's number. 'Could that be our Freddie, Sudhakaran?'

I did not have the patience for a preface.

'I think so too.' Sudhakaran sounded exhausted. Caught on the slippery slope of random memories, he was silent for a while before he spoke again.

'That day, though we searched all over the forest, we could not find him either . . .'

The great emptiness left behind by Freddie's disappearance entrenched itself between us, filling our poignant pauses. Certain desolations have the depth of unpaid debts. They can drag you into the past and sadistically reopen the wounds. As I stood enduring that blistering hurt, I asked myself: who was Freddie to us?

I could conceive him only as a physical manifestation of his self. Beyond the outward appearance of the body, the owner himself remains unaware of its inner workings. Just like the bearer of the heart never sees it with his own eyes, all the members of our gang failed to recognize what was at Freddie's core. Whatever it was, it went on throbbing, never revealing itself. When it went missing, we felt bereft of our own heartbeats.

Even though we were his most intimate friends, how come we had never understood Freddie?

We were short-sighted and saw his trips to the forest as the mere hobby of a student. But the faraway forest was his obsession and the time spent there his intoxication.

When Freddie purchased high-end 30*30 Vanguard binoculars, costing $85, to observe the distant beauty of the forest and its birds, we had mocked him. He carried the binoculars always, strapped around his neck—a beloved organ like the heart. His innocuous curiosity about birds had slowly morphed into an obsession, and he joined the birdwatching club that was undertaking a census of birds.

We too had tagged along, keen to be part of any new adventure. We had playfully referred to those forest trips as the 'vanavasa' of the Pandavas.

A guide came along with our fellowship of five as we trekked across the deep forest frequented by rare birds. Freddie would question him about the history and geography of the forested areas. Soon, he became a repository of all knowledge about the forest. His was a strange union with the forest that none of us could comprehend. Freddie never perceived anything forbidding in the deep. That was how a fearless nature developed in him to venture out alone into the mysterious forest

Freddie entered the forest like a formally appointed envoy. He hugged the Bodhi trees, surrounded by termite hills, as if they were close relatives. Through the lens, he watched the birds and animals that reigned in the forests. And he showed us the swiftness of the twite, the crown of the red-whiskered bulbul, the diving prowess of the darter, the headstand of the short-nosed fruit bat. Once, he waxed eloquent on the idiosyncrasies of the red-wattled lapwing.

'The haughty fellow thinks that he is the one holding the sky in its place! Even when he's asleep, his claws are turned towards the sky, preventing the sky from falling on our heads! He protects us even in his sleep.'

Thus, Freddie would unravel the freaky habits of birds whose names were unfamiliar to us. It was not just birdwatching that captivated him, but the architecture of nests. His view was that all branches of engineering were inspired by nature.

Once Freddie discovered a great Indian hornbill's nest inside the hollow of a tree trunk. It was a rare find, a treasure, and it made him ecstatic. Using the balls of earth the male bird brought, added to her own body wastes, the female had shut the entrance to her home. Only her bill extended out through a slit. We observed, from our hiding places, how the male bird fed the female who was busy hatching eggs, bringing her food frequently. Love for the unseen partner reflected in the male bird's eyes.

'Did you eat something?' 'Is it going to rain soon?' 'What shall we name our children?' Perhaps that was the gist of their chirpings. Freddie did not have the heart to turn his back on that innocent love. Though he wanted to stay another eight days to watch the female bird break open the closure and peep out from her nest, we persuaded him to return with us. However, unknown to us, Freddie did return on the ninth day and was witness to that exquisite vision. That was the first evidence we got of Freddie's unalloyed nature. It was also an indicator of how deeply touched he was by sights that the majority of people shrugged off as trivial.

Freddie would whoop, like a sailor discovering a new continent, whenever he discovered a rare species of bird.

In the intermediate period, when he could not visit the forest as he wished, Freddie once confessed to me that he heard the haunting call of a bird, as yet undiscovered in the Sahyadri ranges, beckoning him regularly. I found the idea of a forest bird calling out to a city man inexplicable.

'Bird-crazy fool!'

Though I ridiculed him for his strange proclivity, Freddie continued to hear the invisible bird's invitation.

'Perhaps it took flight from within me and proceeded to the deep forests,' Freddie quipped. 'One day, I shall seek it out myself.'

What was that birdsong that he heard which was not audible to us? I do not know, but it was true that Freddie would never lie. He strove to do every deed—even those which were not entirely decent—with utmost sincerity. He was never lackadaisical and was extremely alert even in conducting the bird census. The charts were meticulous and denoted how many times a bird species had been sighted in the forests. We were not too impressed by his methodology of categorizing birds as per sound, colour and behaviour. But Freddie was adamant that the charts be as accurate as possible, even if they included superfluous information.

In Freddie's perspective, it was easy to exhibit honesty externally and tough to be truthful to one's own self. Only then could one be honest with nature.

And that was the lone way to the first or primary phase of nature.

Like anyone with common sense would, we too viewed Freddie's insight about the first phase of nature as a mere aberration. Hence, we could not accept his bird love, entangled in multiple charts, with the intensity it deserved. We never bothered to flip through the books of Salim Ali and Hans Mortensen that were in Freddie's room. What was the point of reading about birds when we lacked time even to read thick books on engineering? But Freddie put aside the technical tomes and pecked around the secrets of birds in those books.

That was how Freddie became entranced by the nests woven by the bowerbirds of Papua New Guinea and visiting those sites became one of his life goals. He added, albeit to appease us, that the nests stirred his curiosity not as a birdwatcher alone but as a civil engineer too. What he disclosed about bowerbird's nest fascinated us too.

Apparently, the 3-metre-tall love-nest the bowerbird made was an architectural marvel! Thousands of twigs were arranged to make the 'love bower', which was then covered with couch grass by the male bird. There was a separate birthing room for the female to lay eggs and hatch them. Next to that, a dance floor paved with attractive pebbles. The male was versatile in charming his female, from his engineering design to his dancing skills. Once the fledglings hatched, the parents joined them in iridescent dance moves. If the tale was enough to enrapture even someone like me, who was not predisposed towards the forests, how smitten would Freddie have been with it!

Freddie, who was first beguiled by an intriguing bird, was one day seduced by the forest. It soon had him in its grip and enchanted him with splendours undisclosed to others.

It was after Freddie's disappearance, while perusing the diary in his hostel room, that we learnt of that hidden part in him. That day, we heard the birdsong that had relentlessly

pursued Freddie right from the Sahyadri mountain ranges.
It was then that the secret, which either Freddie had hidden
from us or we had ignored carelessly, was revealed. Like
every late arrival, the diary noting remained a useless
keepsake in my custody. Had it reached me beforehand, I
might have prevented Freddie from ending up as a mere
newspaper article.

Ruminating over the incidents in an untrammelled manner,
I concluded that Sudhakaran too would be doing the same—
mulling over the sequence of incidents which had coalesced
into the news item. Our thoughts, traversing through different
paths, confronted one another in due course.

If the newspaper article was correct, another expedition
to Pullothikkadu was necessary. If we travelled through the
pages of Freddie's diary, a forest path might open up before us.
Following the secret that made the forest take possession of a
human being, we might reach Freddie himself. If so, the forest
would witness another oddity: the reclaiming of a forest man
by civilization.

'Since this thought has occurred to us both, shall we check
with the rest, Sudhakaran?' I asked. My question was provoked
by the fact that the five of us could not be separated from
one another.

'Definitely,' Sudhakaran replied. 'Then you should call
Muhammad Rafi first.'

Rafi was the Nakula in the Pandava fellowship. He had the
looks and physique of a movie star. Along with the name of
a famous playback singer, the man possessed singing prowess
too. For three years in a row, he had won prizes for singing
in the university youth festivals. Freddie made him sing the
beloved songs from the movie *Dosti* often.

I called up Rafi alias Nakula.

He hadn't read the news yet. Rafi was asleep from fatigue; he'd given an interview in Bangalore the previous day and returned by bus very late in the night.

As soon as he heard the news, Rafi became distraught.

He had always been like that. Very sensitive. The agitation caused by Freddie Robert's disappearance had been incendiary, affecting Rafi the most. He had been a village boy, untouched by the vagaries of city life. He would never have voluntarily joined the Pandava group.

Freddie had decided everything.

I had presumed that Rafi wouldn't readily accept the idea of yet another forest trip. But he was enthusiastic. He retained intense regrets over an unfulfilled pact with Freddie. It was after the final separation from Freddie that Rafi had become anxious about it.

Neither did Rafi disclose what the secret pact was, nor did I probe further.

The person left for me to contact was the Bhimasena of the Pandava group: Sahadeva Iyer. Since there was no telephone in Iyer's home, I was forced to call up a neighbour, requesting that a message be passed on that Iyer was to get in touch. Iyer belonged to a poor family and his employment was crucial for their sustenance. Freddie always had a soft corner for Iyer's struggles.

Iyer called back around noon. After lunch, I was lying in my room and contemplating the past again. Some vignettes in blue, like impressions in carbon copies.

'Mahesh! Are you sure it is Freddie?' Iyer asked frantically. His voice was always fraught with tension.

'Considering that we lost him in that area . . .'

The prospect of travelling to Pullothikkadu again intimidated Iyer. His body was huge, but his mind was timid

and hesitant. The disaster wrought by the last forest trip still
had him in its clutches.

I had to venture forth like a mediator, trying to establish
peace between Iyer and the forest. After listening to the 'Kaliyug
Gita' that Arjuna had narrated to Bhima, Iyer acquiesced.

It was when the four of us decided to start off in search of
the eldest of the Pandavas that Iyer raised a pertinent query and
hurled me into the whirlpools it created.

'Mahesh! What about Meera? Our Panchali?'

'Will she come?'

'Try calling her.'

'I don't think so. When she was in college, it was different.
Now that she is at home after her degree, how will she convince
her family?'

The relationship that Meera had with the Pandavas was
a secret that had been betrayed to her family early on. She
had been warned to desist from the friendship, and had been
warned about the likelihood of noxious aspersions being cast.
Even a phone call could trigger a catastrophe.

Yet, Iyer insisted.

'Whether she comes or not, she should be informed about
about the journey.'

I felt his advice should not be dismissed.

I dialled Meera's number, ready to cut the call if anyone
other than her were to pick up.

I didn't need to execute the plan; Meera picked up the
phone herself.

Even before I could elaborate on the trip, she agreed to
step into the uncertainties of the forest.

'How can any vanavasa be complete without Panchali? We
lost Freddie in the last trip because I was not there with you.
Now I feel damn sure that I will be the one to find him.'

For that advantage alone, I was willing to go along with any feminine obstinacy. Would we truly be able to reach out to Freddie and bring him back to life?

'You must have Freddie's diary with you. Don't forget to bring it along,' Meera reminded me before disconnecting the call.

On the third day, the four of us set off in search of the fifth member of the group, along with Meera S. Nair, the one who might be hailed in history as the bravest girl in the engineering college.

As directed by Meera, when I placed Freddie's diary inside my bag, its heartbeats pulsated on my fingers.

2

ARJUNA

As I boarded the bus to the city, my mind was turbulent with many thoughts. Like a lunatic, cutting off all restraining strings, it wandered through the pathways I had traversed with Freddie Robert.

A night of thunderstorms, when a gulmohar tree had crashed into Freddie's east-facing hostel room, struck me with force. The omen in the crashing tree was more comprehensible to me now than before. There was a link between the uprooting of the tree and Freddie's self-imposed silence.

It was our final year in the engineering college. Freddie Robert, who was a year senior to us, had continued in the fellowship of the Pandavas because he had lost a year due to rustication. We often felt that his aim was not the degree granted at the end of the technical education. Just passing the course was good enough for him. He would study hard a day or two before the examinations and achieve this goal. We were far more fascinated by the wayward 'technical games' he often indulged in. But one could not afford those peccadilloes in the last year of engineering studies. We were racking our brains on how to reduce the extracurricular activities of the Pandava fellowship when the premature demise of the gulmohar occurred on that windy and rainy night.

Freddie's room, which was in the corner of the hostel where gulmohar had fallen, was devastated. It was only due to his solitary forest trip that he had miraculously escaped the disaster. If he had not felt like proceeding without us, his death would have been certain that night.

When Freddie returned, he stood brooding silently at the sight of his devastated sanctuary. Then he spoke, as if to himself: 'One Freddie has died.'

That simple sentence struggled to withstand the weight of its own import.

He spoke like someone who viewed his own death with indifference. His solitary sojourn had stolen something profound from him. Or it had showered him generously with something else. Regardless of what had transpired, a relentless guilt started pursuing us for having let him go off alone into the forests. We were not brave enough to miss classes and participate in that trip when the examinations were imminent. Yet, none of us had stopped the journey or told him that we would not be going along. We simply dropped broad hints about the gravity of the final year.

'That is right,' Freddie acknowledged, 'one has to be very careful when nearing the end.'

And the next morning, without saying goodbye to anyone, he had left for the forests with his Vanguard binoculars. If the forest had not beckoned him that day, a life would have been sacrificed under the uprooted tree. Perhaps the forest that Freddie trusted so implicitly had saved him. Or perhaps, his trust had been fortified because the forest had saved him. But it remains a mystery till today how the healthy gulmohar had given way unexpectedly, toppling over and into the room. Our fellowship had spent countless nights relishing the enchantment of Mohammed Rafi's songs beneath that tree. By the time we made our way back to the hostel rooms to roost, it would be dawn.

The hostel was designed with constructions on four sides and a yard at the centre. It was in this square yard that we conducted the annual hostel-day celebrations. The warden allotted a room in the opposite corner for Freddie, to recompense for the ruined room. The five of us foraged through the remains of the erstwhile room for Freddie's possessions. We discarded whatever was useless and shifted the rest to the new room.

This new room of Freddie's was far away from mine. The separation of the single wall which had existed between us earlier, convoluted into the distance of multiple walls and corners. Mostly, Freddie would spend long hours of the night in my room, transgressing the boundary set by the wall. Of the five, he was closest to me. Hence the unforeseen 'room separation' from Freddie Robert caused me anxiety. When he did not appear in my room, as was his wont, I set off for his new room in search of the friendship that had gone amiss.

Freddie was busy scribbling something in his diary.

'What are you so busy writing about?' I asked.

'Hey, nothing,' he shrugged listlessly.

Freddie continued to write as if unaffected by my presence. God, it took me too long to discover the power of those words that he had written that day!

It was while searching his room after losing him in the forest that the writings with their scalding contents ended up in my hands. It hurts me even now that though I was but inches away from him while he wrote, so many losses had to be endured before discerning the truth behind his words.

It soon became evident that hidden secrets were deeper than those disclosed. Freddie started distancing himself from everybody and everything. We became apprehensive about whatever was happening between Freddie and us, causing that wilful shutdown. Though we invited him for a nightly sojourn— typical for us when studies bored us—Freddie declined. Stealing a tapioca or jackfruit from a neighbourhood compound, encroaching into forbidden territories for the fun of it, jumping across the wall of the ladies' hostel to showcase our prowess— these were all intrinsic parts of our nightly adventures.

Though he was rotund, Iyer was the one who excelled in the art of jumping over the wall of the ladies' hostel. Throwing away his mundu, and dressed only in his underwear, he would clamber up the water pipe to reach the open window. Shining his torch in, he would gaze to his fill at the sumptuous sight of the sleeping beauties. The mechanical engineering student Sahadeva Iyer's horsepower sprung from the wicked desire of glimpsing some flesh revealed under an awry dress or two. He would grieve openly about the lack of women in his class and express his vain hopes of joining either civil engineering or computer science as a solution.

Iyer's sleep vanished due to the attractive posterior of Kartika Rajendran, the civil engineering beauty. Her undulating walking style was famously termed SHM— Simple Harmonic Motion— in the college. Iyer's ambition of watching the pendulum swing in its original beauty provoked him into many nightly capers. The initials before his name, like a prior promise, were 'LH'. Maybe his ancestors' blessings were that he was destined to cross the wall of the LH— Ladies' Hostel!

Once, L.H. Sahadeva Iyer ascended the drainage pipe to test out a new mechanical technique. He extended a stick, which had been duly dipped in the gum of jackfruit, and touched the skirt of the 'civil' beauty. As the skirt slowly lifted up, Kartika Rajendran woke up. At the sight of the underwear-clad figure at the window, she screamed and Iyer, with his flabby body, frantically slithered down the pipe, raced towards the wall and somehow made his escape by scaling the wall.

The aftermath was that a watchman nicknamed 'Komban' aka 'Tusker' appeared in the ladies' hostel the next day! Iyer became too scared to sneak inside the hostel, guarded by a billhook-wielding Komban.

To surmount Iyer's formidable obstacle, Freddie Robert trounced the 'tusker' with liquor. During one such night, Sahadeva Iyer got ready to scale the hostel wall yet again. Later, Iyer proclaimed that his leap from the wall to the ladies' hostel compound took as long as the one from the sky to the earth, with him floating in the air for a long time before his feet touched the ground. After much air travel, it was when he landed in a slushy pit, that he discovered the trap. Hearing the resounding thud, the lights in the ladies' hostel blazed. Though the inmates hollered 'Komban, Komban', the watchman did not wake, as a result of the tranquilizer shot. Freddie and the rest of us somehow managed to save Sahadeva Iyer; it was like hauling up a wild elephant from the pit! This pit later became renowned in the engineering college as 'The L.H. Iyer Memorial Pit'.

It was another matter altogether that Freddie Robert proved that Iyer, despite his escapades, was a coward in the matter of women! Not just Iyer, almost all the hostel inmates, though attempting some light adventures, never indulged in any immoral activities.

We were greatly perplexed when Freddie Robert suddenly lost interest in such extracurricular aberrations. With no sign of the anxiety that besets final-year students, he started ignoring classes. He stopped coming to the hostel mess in time, disturbing his eating habits. It was a self-imposed solitary confinement in the new room.

When friendship became incarcerated thus, it started affecting our Pandava fellowship the most. A situation arose where the sky-high edifice of the House of Pandavas looked likely crash to the ground, leaving nothing behind.

More than anyone else, Freddie Robert had made arduous efforts in formulating a fellowship with a series of rules and sustaining it with his sheer life-force. He was the Yudhishtira who had discovered us from here and there. The one who let us trail along like his brothers, allowed us to thrive under his wisdom and money, who poured out for us the intoxicating wild flower brew.

Like a peacock dosing on opium, we could not suddenly separate from the institution to which we had been stuck. It was our responsibility as friends to bring him back to life in case his mind had been ensnared by a deviant fantasy.

But that required caution.

Freddie Robert's actions were unpredictable.

The elusive truth was that we could not fathom what went on inside him, despite having been intimate friends for almost four years. Though the rest of us were familiar with each other's families, Freddie's family details remained cryptic, like the secret of an unopened ark. From his name, one could surmise that his father was a Robert. From some kingdom belonging to the Lord of Wealth, uncountable money came in search of him. He spent it on his Pandava siblings without any reservations.

We could not adjust to our sudden descent from such heights. For us, it was rather a belated realization that not just Yudhishtira, but Arjuna, Bhima and the sons of Madri, all had been sustaining themselves only on Freddie Robert's strength. None of us could match up to him in any field.

In the absence of Freddie, we were zilch.

The concept of Indraprastha became redundant.

Consequently, even while in class, my compatriots and I were anxious about the one who had committed himself to a solitary existence in his hostel room. When our anxiety sharpened, we decided to pay him a visit when no one else was around in the hostel. The plan was that I would slip out after marking my attendance in Rama Warrier sir's thermal engineering class; the others would meet me by the lab. That day, the blackboard was clamouring with Cyclical Integral Functions. For the last few days, Rama Warrier sir had been struggling to make us understand 'that entropy was the order of disorder', writing down the equation that the cyclic integral of dQ/T was always less than or equal to zero. But there was no order to the disorder inside me.

I received the signal that the other three had assembled at the window behind the class. Escaping Rama Warrier sir's class was as easy as floating a bit of Indian milkwood. His soda bottle-thick spectacles could not observe the people on the earth clearly. Some were escaping, jumping like frogs near the rostrum where he stood; Rama Warrier sir continued to go mechanically through the equations of thermodynamics. In the front bench were a few knowledge-thirsty dimwits with open mouths and frozen bodies! But they never received marks equal to their endurance.

As the cyclical integral progressed on the blackboard, retreating from that equation, I jumped out through the window. Even if every student left the class, Rama Warrier sir's class would continue uninterrupted.

We proceeded towards the Heat Engines Laboratory situated behind the college. There was a vast cashew plantation behind it. Red and yellow cashew fruits dangled ripe in the trees.

It was Sudhakaran who started the conversation, saying that many had enquired about Freddie that day.

'Same here,' Muhammad Rafi said. 'We have to find some way out.'

'Mahesh, I feel you should meet him as our representative,' Iyer opined.

'Why? He is equally approachable to all of us!'

'Better that you go. He might open up more to you.'

We construed that even if he kept away from all other external contacts, Freddie would have a soft corner for the fellowship. And that was how, as the representative of the four of us, and also as the closest to Freddie Robert, I was appointed as the emissary for a conciliatory meeting.

It was on that day that Freddie's innermost padlocks opened wondrously before me.

3

FACE TO FACE

Out of the blue, dark clouds gathered above the cashew plantation and a heavy wind started blowing. The families of doves, which roosted on the heights of the Heat Engines Lab, scattered around, fluttering, and sought safe haven. The dried mango leaves took flight like a bevy of birds.

'It is going to rain,' Sahadeva Iyer commented, looking at the leaf-birds.

'Then you better go to the hostel before that. We will wait for you behind the lab,' Muhammad Rafi said.

We watched a dove, afraid of the rain, landing on top of the Cochran boiler inside the lab. The roar of the Kirloskar engine began farther down. From among the batches doing various machine tests, one had started the Efficiency Test. The lab was full of blue humans wearing cotton pants and shirts of that colour. They were busy marking the engine capabilities through points and graphs in green-coloured record books.

But what I had to mark was the sample points of a man's vagaries. What would be the nature of the graph known as Freddie Robert that I would depict by joining those dots? A straight line, a parabola . . . would I be able to form a common pattern? Or would Freddie create a new graph hitherto unseen, insubordinate to any natural law?

Keeping the mind's graph paper empty, I moved towards the hostel.

There was a huge ground, made by hacking away a hill, between the college and the hostel which I had to cross. White madar bloomed on the sides. Whenever I passed that way, I would be hit by nostalgic childhood memories of using those flowers as markers in boardgames. There was dense undergrowth, with wild creepers entwining thorny trees and fruit-laden clusters of the orangeberry plant. Since I had heard that it was auspicious to plant the orangeberry in front of your home, from the time I joined the engineering college to when I left it after more than four years, I had always wanted to uproot a sapling and had always forgot to follow through on the plan. That plant, with its propitiousness, which never travelled home with me, nevertheless had the company of wild rabbits and mongooses. A short distance away was a place referred to as the 'den of the foxes', and it was inferred that these creatures once roamed in the vicinity.

We, the Pandavas, had stepped across the daunting wild path many times. By rousing the jungle, we had chased down small rabbits. Though we tried to domesticate one such rabbit on the third-floor terrace, it evaded our watch and ended up committing suicide by jumping from the heights.

Our first experience of the forests was a trek through the shrubby jungle near the college. Perhaps it was that mild intoxication which inspired Freddie to seek out the deep forests. An elderly acquaintance had apparently narrated many adventurous tales of his forest travels ever since Freddie was four, thus tempting him. As if engraving the consciousness with an iron stylus, the forest must have enticed him from a young age. Whenever we went to the jungle near the hostel, it was Freddie who led the way with a stick in hand. Cleaving apart thorny shrubs and web-like creepers, he created wild paths that never existed before.

We came to discover that farther along lay a rubber plantation, and on its opposite edge, a canal hidden by clumps of ukshi shrubs. That mass of ukshi made it a perfectly secure, natural hideaway. When the village women stepped into the canal to wash clothes and bathe, they were ignorant of the Pandavas serving their '*ajnata vasa*'—the period of hiding—behind the ukshi clusters.

Moving farther, we too would bathe in the canal. Then, Sahadeva Iyer would be in ecstatic throes, remembering the lush bodies he had voyeuristically surveyed from the sanctuary of the shrubs. He marvelled that the water, having brushed against us, flowed downstream to touch those feminine bodies; the knowledge electrified his senses and made him go berserk. In his metaphor, the stream of water had become an extended condom connecting both male and female nakedness.

Once, when we walked through the rubber plantation after a bath in the canal, Iyer said, 'Today, I have sent my semen on a journey through the water. Perhaps some virgin will conceive from it!'

'A divine pregnancy!' Freddie Robert burst out guffawing.

'Don't laugh,' said Iyer peevishly. 'In our Puranas, you will find many sages who ejaculated on seeing bathing scenes! The divine semen ended up impregnating wombs and many valiant men were created!'

'Just imagine! The heart touching scene when Iyer leaves after four years of engineering studies, and hordes of village belles arrive with babies to bid farewell!'

Our roar of laughter spliced the silence of the rubber plantation.

The rubber grove was fraught with a whimpering sadness. Each rubber tree, with the pain of the unhealed lesion on its heart, seemed to be staring with anguished eyes. For me, the trees, carrying wounds, were a disturbing sight. When the oozing white blood congealed in the dangling waste pouches, they brought to mind patients shorn of life.

However, we could not continue the journeys through the rubber grove and hide under the ukshi shrubs for long. The loose-tongued Iyer babbled about the loveliness of the village maidens in the hostel. That led to a sudden spurt in the population near the canal which the ukshi clumps couldn't conceal, provoking the locals.

That incident led to a skirmish between the villagers and the hostellers, who baptized any depravity with the slogan 'Engineering unity'. The ukshi shrubs were hewn and set afire.

'We are hereby discarding such undesirable trips,' Freddie Robert announced. Then he added with a mysterious grin, 'Why bother about peeking surreptitiously? Whoever wishes to watch directly and experience by touch, may raise their hands!'

Hardly had he heard it when Iyer raised both his hands high!

We thought that Freddie was being bombastic. Having a woman to 'experience by touch' was a luxurious sin and a deadly terror in our adolescence, which had not been corrupted much. Yet, on a night when the hostel was dozing, Freddie Robert knocked at our door, stunning us stupid.

'Whoever will not get burnt on touching a woman is invited to the ground.'

Scared out of my wits, I never ventured anywhere near the ground. I saw a quavering Sahadeva Iyer accompany Freddie Robert. The next day he disclosed to me that he hadn't dared to go beyond some preliminaries.

'What about Freddie?' I asked.

'Didn't do anything at all. Seemed to remove himself from the scene after arranging everything!'

Freddie was always like that. After ensuring that his Pandava siblings' desires were satiated, he would stay detached. The same person, who was always a step ahead, was now cutting himself off from everything.

As I crossed half of that compound's enormity, the rain fell. I raced across the other half and entered the portico before walking to Freddie's room.

The rain-drenched friendship was welcomed with a hearty smile. To lessen the tension, I started yammering about irrelevant stuff. As I skimmed through the superfluities of college news, I was wondering when to change course dexterously. Like a fool I spouted about how a cockroach was found in the mess food and how Rosily De'cruz had slipped down the staircase. My situation was akin to checking the reactions of the engine in the Heat Engine Lab, conducting an efficiency test by increasing and decreasing the RPM or the rotations per minute. At an opportune juncture, I hinted about the common anxiety regarding his absence from class. Outside, there were rain and wind at that moment, and in the room just me and Freddy.

Unexpectedly, when Freddie Robert came closer and lifted up my chin, the RPM of the machine inside me increased, and unable to convert it into straight-line motions, my heart trembled.

'You have been sent as an envoy, right?'

I was in a condition where I could neither refute nor accept his query. Freddie responded in his typical style of serenely dealing with such situations. 'I named you Arjuna, didn't I?' Freddie Robert asked.

'Yes,' I answered, though there was no need to.

'Master Archer whose aim never falters, tell me, what will you do when your mind loses aim?'

As I stood gaping, unable to comprehend his question, Freddie Robert looked deep into my eyes and asked, 'Let me rephrase. Why do you attend classes?'

Even as I floundered, unable to gauge the question, Freddie had the air of not expecting any answer. His expression was solemn and tranquil. Then he sketched my goals clearer than I could.

'Studies, job, hefty salary, a prized matrimony based on all the preceding . . . Am I right?'

Though I hadn't pondered that far, since Freddie Robert's statement contained some home truths, I didn't bother to counter him. The breeze, which entered the room with the scent of rain, cast a silence between us and circled around, puzzling over what was coming next.

Freddie had always loved the fragrance of the rain.

He breathed in deeply, standing next to the window.

'But I don't have any such goals, Arjuna. Why build a bow when you've nowhere to aim your arrow? Why check the size and strength of your bowstring? The stress and strain that we study in "Strength of Materials" are no longer relevant for me. Today, I define a human as a tube of flesh, a few kilometres in elongation. Why doesn't this knowledge, that we are merely a long tube connecting the mouth and the excretory orifice, fill us with loathing? See, I am elucidating because of the human weakness of wanting at least one person to understand you. If you don't understand me, no one else can! I . . . I no longer need any artifice!'

'What . . . what is the artifice here, Freddie?'

'Isn't everything artificial? Is it after studying about the first battle of Panipat and Sher Shah's administrative reforms that the fisherman catches fish and you eat them? If one doesn't know about the Pythagoras theorem or the Fourier series, will the rice fields stop yielding a harvest? What's the use of studying those books and scientific laws, which are never going to be useful and which aren't supposed to be useful? Tell me, are you a satisfied person?'

'Satisfaction is a relative experience, Freddie. One has to find it where one stands.'

'You said it! All that I gained for my satisfaction, no longer satisfies me. Those who hear it will denounce it as madness. But I am obsessed with this madness. Mahesh, I cannot help it. I want to perform an extreme act of daring . . . extreme!'

I did not know this Freddie.

I had been thrilled by Freddie's glorious antics. He gave a dramatic twist to any straightforward action. Now his outrageous self-assurance had grown to such heights as to challenge life itself!

Inadvertently, I asked, 'There is an Indraprastha that we established. What will happen to that, Freddie?'

'Arjuna, you are mistaken if you have established Indraprastha in your mind! Shortly, all of us will get out of this temporary retreat. The five Pandavas and Panchali will be scattered wide. What of Yudhishtira then? What Indraprastha? Before that I want to join the first phase of nature.'

'First phase?' I asked bemused. 'When did nature begin to have phases?'

'See,' Freddie said, 'the only covering I have is the towel around my waist. Until I heard the knock on the door, I was free even of that! I can no longer walk around with an ironed, overstrung mind. No longer can I take sides with any relativity. Neither right and wrong, nor good and bad, nor day and night. Like a mountaineer finds his dress and footwear burdensome, the same is with me. Both separate me from myself. Even this cement floor that I stand on is so artificial! In nature's first phase, there is no cement mix or concrete roof. There is neither past nor future. Only an unrestrained present.'

'That means . . .' I spoke hesitantly, 'some sort of wild animal . . . unable to think.'

Unprovoked, Freddie smiled serenely at me.

'Only the forest has a pure present time. The one who can live like a wild animal, after understanding himself, is fortunate. Without worrying about what is behind him, and without concerning himself with what is yet to come, he can exist peacefully in the present.'

Never had I expected such a strong turnaround from Freddie. As if the forest trips and birdwatching had created an ancient, Neanderthal man! Unless he was convinced, Freddie would never change like this. I felt that one had to take him to a psychiatrist, to reclaim him from that conviction. A psychiatrist who specialized in anti-nature therapy!

I was becoming tired of the dingy arguments unsuitable to the leader of the Pandava fellowship. Perchance it was the temporary ennui of a man who had satiated himself to the utmost with the luxuries of life which made him speak thus. But I hadn't yet relished life at that level. Since I could only contemplate what was left to conquer, I neither wanted to, nor could I understand, the transmuting of Freddie.

I noticed that the diary with the brown cover in which Freddie had scribbled long into the night, after returning from his trip, was lying on the table. The belief that it contained many secrets strengthened in me. But that diary was not fated to end up in my hands until we had lost him in the forest!

'What are you busy thinking about?' Freddie asked. 'Wondering who is the foremost psychiatrist in town?'

He laughed loudly after effortlessly dragging out my innermost rumination.

'My friend, the first phase of nature is not of interest to a psychiatrist. It is the first primeval calling of the human race. We all have it, to different degrees. It's just that we cover it up with variegated covers and pretend to be modern. A man, uncovered, is the same anywhere in the world.'

As I stood devastated, my mind's shores wrecked by a furious wave of thoughts, Freddie continued, 'An insane person cannot recognize his own lunacy. But I have a good idea of what you guys think of me! If you cannot appreciate my perspective, it is nobody's fault. Because, in this world, there are certain unique experiences. Maybe I am different from the rest. Would you have arrived with your missive today had I been killed by that toppling gulmohar? Mahesh, what is better? A dead man or a wild man? If I am allowed to choose, I would vote for the wild man . . .'

Freddie Robert had padlocked my mouth, disallowing any repudiation. My mission had ended in a horrendous calamity.

Then, Freddie came close to me and putting his hand over my shoulder, spoke: 'Tell the members of the fellowship that I haven't forgotten them. We shall visit Pullothikkadu once more before parting.'

Unable to accept the abruptness of that promise, I glared at him. In that situation, his words were too onerous for me to absorb.

'Let's fix it for next Saturday. Since Monday is a holiday, you will not miss your classes.'

With the glad news of a successful mission, I rushed like an engine towards those awaiting me behind the Heat Engines Lab. The overspeeding augmented the engine's heartbeats.

The Kirloskar was silent, having overcome the efficiency test. In its place, the growl of a diesel engine was shaking the surroundings. Neither my compatriots nor I knew that the diesel engine was trumpeting our final journey with Freddie.

4

BHIMASENA

It was Freddie who hacked off my identity by naming me 'Bhimasena'. Although the first naming was unintentional, it stuck with me as if preordained by fate.

I would certainly have desisted from acting that part had I any forewarning of the malfeasance waiting to spread.

Today, I regret travelling through the forbidden, which we are supposed to abstain from and which no student should dare contemplate.

Liquor, meat, woman . . .

The singular reason that I let the inner animal in me roam over pastures which were at once munificent and perverse for an impecunious youth, was the senior student, Freddie Robert.

But I hold no grudges against Freddie. Only an envious approbation. Perhaps it would be better to say that I was willing to be misled, than that he misled me.

It was Freddie Robert's riches which protected me from the severe shortcomings of acute poverty. The inferiority caused by indigence, which had assailed me relentlessly from childhood, fought utmost with Freddie and finally ended through him.

I had no clue about a technical education when I reached the hostel of the engineering college, with a leather bag that my father had procured by begging the neighbourhood. The bag contained some old clothes and oddities. Due to its age, the edges and handle were discoloured, as if infected with vitiligo. As soon as I reached the hostel, with the symbols which showcased my destitution, someone with reddish eyes and close-cropped hair came to welcome me.

'Welcome, gentleman. What's your name?'

'Sahadeva Iyer,' I said, flustered by his unexpected intervention.

'Sahadeva Iyer. Good! Let us drop the Iyer. What's left is "Sahadeva". But you have the look of Bhimasena. That's it, your name shall be Bhimasena from today. Is that clear?'

'Yes, clear.'

'What's clear?'

'That my name is Bhimasena.'

I did not know then that the man interacting with me was a second-year student called Freddie Robert or that I would be nicknamed 'Bhimasena' for the next four years.

What stood out on his face was a weird cruelty and a seething contempt for the world. He had the looks and nature of a sadist.

In a jiffy, Freddie Robert's nature transformed.

'Pbha! Son of a mongrel! What did you plan to study here? Where did you get this stinking coffin from? Got it by begging?'

Remembering my father, fighting with his recalcitrant lungs inside the narrow room of our home, I accepted with servility the title of 'son of a mongrel'.

'My Appa borrowed it from the neighbour.'

When I revealed the truth of the coffin, Freddie Robert's face flushed with repugnance. By that time, some others had joined in to poke fun at my pathos.

'Heard that? Beggars and cobblers have started studying engineering! How will our land progress?'

The cronies relished the spicy jest and roared with laughter.

'But how did a beggar get so fat? You steal food, don't you?'

It was true that there was a scarcity of food in my household. Though my hunger was not satiated, my body hid its inner shortcomings smartly and exhibited its bounty externally. As I stood brooding over the illimitable largesse granted by my body, Freddie enunciated some soothing words.

'Poor thing! You must be tired holding the bag. Please put it down.'

It was true.

My joints were aching from continuously holding it. As I tried to straighten up after putting the bag down, another harsh command thundered.

'Pbha, rascal! Haul it up on to your head!'

I lost my sense of direction.

My brain declared non-cooperation, and the thoughts were stymied. As another threat boomed nearby, I stood like a manual labourer with the bag on my head.

'Never make me repeat an instruction. Now get going!'

Carrying the burden on my head, I walked aimlessly, remembering the family deity in the attic, thinking of my asthmatic father and the helplessness of my siblings.

I counted each burning step as pushing me far away from life. He was making me march towards the senior students' hostel. When I recollected the brutal stories of ragging, my feet became numb.

At that moment, as if the invisible hand of the family deity had touched my head, a voice sounded from behind.

'Enough, enough. Now put your bag down and proceed to the warden's room. Don't you want to know which room has been allotted to you?'

The sudden relief from that atmosphere of terror astounded me a bit. The aggrievement on being baptized as Bhimasena slipped away, and shed its skin. For a moment, I even admired the man with bloodshot eyes who had restored to me whatever I thought was lost. He possessed the commanding demeanour to lead a fellowship. Only, the cruelty flaring in the eyes could have been lesser.

The room allotted to me was Room Number 21.

Climbing the steps and reaching the first floor, it turned out to be the first room to the left. There were rookies like me there, disconcerted and petrified. The first thing to seize my attention was the window looking east. One had an aerial view of the front grounds. The names of the erstwhile inmates were scribbled with chalk on the ceiling made from conjoined wooden planks. If this was the practice, I was destined to have my name on the list.

The rule was that there would be four first-year students in one room. It was a three-person sharing system for the second year, and by the final year turned to single occupancy.

There were four wooden cots in the room where the 'Worldwide Conference of Bedbugs' was taking place. Regardless of darkness or light, the bedbugs assaulted whichever body pressed down on them. The respite was that the bloodthirsty, monstrous mosquitoes only visited at night. When the mosquitoes tried to fly away with the body, it was helpful that the bug bites acted as a counter force, pinning one down to the bed. The body would remain like zero: the resultant of opposing forces.

Since the first few months of the new students were a probation period, the group headed by Freddie Robert enlightened us on the rites to be followed. The main rule on apparel was that pants were a strict no-no. Only a single *mundu* and shirt were allowed. There was an absolute ban on underwear. One could leave the hostel only after confirming that particular security protocol. Wearing footwear was an egregious violation of the law.

These were the physical efficiency tests for undergoing a tough technical education. To ensure no escalation of arrogance, one had to offer the engineering salute to the seniors and accept their superiority. It was an unforgiveable sin to make any mistake in the said technology, which comprised holding and shaking one's manhood in the left hand while saluting with the right.

Freddie Robert taught us Newton's Fourth Law of Motion on the very first day. Apparently, this was developed in the engineering college under special grant of the government.

The thrust of breasts is directly proportional to the product of masses of breasts and inversely proportional to the square of the distance between the nipples.

When I unwittingly grinned, thinking of the humour in multiplying the masses of two breasts and dividing them by the square of the distance between the nipples, a blow landed squarely on my neck.

'Leering, eh, Bhima?'

Thus, Freddie Robert became the donor of the very first corporal punishment I endured in my life. The shock of its impact travelled from behind the neck to the head, and many unseen places shuddered.

I was unaware that the initial blow was simply the announcement of many more to follow. Of one thing I was sure: there was no alternative but to shrivel into the shell of one's insecure existence and display total subservience.

The menu in the hostel mess at 4 p.m. was boiled plantains. Due to extreme hunger and exhaustion, as I ravenously unpeeled the plantain, Freddie Robert's unassailable warning ensued.

'Leave the plantains on the plate and eat only the skins, you wretched livestock!'

Even then we did not realize that a situation worse than what cattle faced was lying in wait for us. One guy drove us with a stick towards the senior hostel. We were forced to be four-legged creatures, crawling up the three flights of stairs on our knees, kissing every step on the way. As I struggled to climb, kissing the stairs, the cart driver kicked my butt from behind and hollered.

'Why so lazy after stuffing yourself with banana skins, you bovine?'

Forgetting all difficulties, I speedily clambered up to the top floor at one go. That journey ended in a vast corner room on that floor.

Each one of us had to step into that room alone. In the passage ahead, under the leadership of Freddie Robert, a gang was interviewing every person.

One of them waved a device that resembled a metal-detector over my body and it suddenly started beeping danger signals.

Kkrniim—kkrniim—kkrniim . . .

As I panicked at that unanticipated alarm, Freddie Robert roared, 'Have you hidden some bomb somewhere? Or some deadly weapon?'

I shook my head to indicate 'no'.

'Does that mean the detector has lied? We should know the truth! Remove your shirt.'

Distraught, I removed my shirt.

'Umm, now remove your mundu!'

When he repeated his order, I gazed at Freddie in utter disbelief. Since the probation period was still on, I was stark naked under that cloth wrapped around my waist.

'What's the delay? Go ahead, quick! Have to discover the deadly weapon you've hidden!'

I was trembling with embarrassment and despair. However, the shells covering the seniors had hardened so deep that they were untouched by my utter helplessness and piteousness.

After delivering a kick, which bruised me mentally more than bodily, one of the gang members shouted, 'Won't obey, you swine? Just wait . . .'

As my hands mechanically stretched to my mundu and I revealed myself, a raucous, celebratory laughter resounded from the gathering. My manhood had shrivelled up in deep terror.

'Oh, was it *this* deadly weapon that you had hidden? Hey Chitragupta, Bookkeeper of Yama, take him away to hell! No clothes, no kindness, no peace there. Only screams and the gnashing of teeth.'

Roughly shoved once more from behind, I stumbled to reach the shut door of the recreation room. Above the door was inscribed 'Hell', with a sign of skull and bones beneath. I felt horrified, as if viewing my own skull and bones.

As the door opened before me, enduring another hard slap, my hellish entry to a place with no clothes, no kindness and no peace became complete.

5

HELL

From the great depths, at times, hell makes an appearance on earth with its fire, brimstone and gnashing of teeth. I saw those who had entered purgatory before me stand blanching like naked souls. Upon a hard shove, I almost hit the ground.

The room completely silent, with no wisp of sound left to filter away. Outside, the sentries were busy with their detector tests and verdicts. The 'Keepers of Hell' entered only after the last naked man had plunged into the room.

'Denizens of Hell,' Freddie Robert's voice rang out, ending the stillness, 'this is the recreation room. Here, the creativity of each and every one shall be examined. That no fucking bastards who disobey shall leave this hell happens to be the law. The first item that you shall present is a hell dance. Chitragupta, kindly play a knockout song so these souls can perform a group dance!'

Chitragupta switched on the record player, initiating a slow rap. As the music played, Freddie commanded: 'Now, start!'

One by one, when others unwillingly started shaking their bodies, I too joined reluctantly. My portly body did not have the flexibility for dancing. I could not keep up with the tempo when the rap beats quickened.

Unsatisfied with my clumsy movements, Freddie Robert snarled.

'C'mon! Fast, everybody.'

The dance turned faster at that. The music started becoming sharper and wilder. Along with the screeches and demonic instruments of the wild men, as the beats became rapid and moved towards a crescendo, we were forced to move our bodies to keep up.

The state of our organs was like cotton balls quivering in a cyclone. At the end of that long, fatiguing dance, I stood panting, with aching thigh joints.

'Now everybody lie down!'

Hardly had the words been spoken than the naked men sprawled on the ground on their tummies. The floor was not wide enough for so many of us to lie at a stretch. Crushed, jostling, groaning, as each found a space for himself, Freddie Robert issued the next order.

'Now comes the return from hell to earth. But there is a convention to follow. Since the hell dwellers are legless, they roll in order to move! Those who roll fast and furious can escape first. It is desirable that you roll over those creating obstructions. I shall not free the last four remaining in the room. They shall be deserving of the toughest punishments in hell.'

I listened to the last sentence with the same trepidation as of touching death. Among those lying stuck to one another, who would be the last four? Not to belong to that group became a necessity. Our heartbeats were loud enough for others to hear.

'Here you go . . . Ready, one, two, three!'

Going against all earthly systems, a group circumambulation began! In the quest to get outside, each tried to roll over the other. With all my strength, I too joined that great flow. The boisterousness of the senior students who were applauding and screaming while savouring the sight, the desperation of those trying to roll and flee, the inner torment at ending as one of the last four . . . my body was not pliable, yet I kept rolling.

Making me its axis, the world started whirling around me. Above me rotated many feet, heads and tummies. Elbows dug into my chest fiercely. My lower stomach was kicked viciously. Realizing that I was lagging behind, I forgot my bruised body and became a mere rotation. Just a spinning which went round and round and round.

My spin knocked against those struggling at the door like flipping fishes. I saw that my face was brushing against two feet, which stood between me and the doorway to escape. Though my body had stopped rolling, the universe whirled with manic energy, and I found myself lying at the feet of someone like a refugee.

'Bhimasena, you are trapped with three others!'

My innards cleaved at Freddie's forewarning.

Along with three other innards.

'Umm, get up!'

On receiving the order, four naked human beings stood up wobbling. I wasn't able to stand straight.

Freddie Robert's arm reached out and grasped my long hair.

'Didn't you know that the hippie generation is over? Chitragupta, pass me the scissors!'

Chitragupta presented the scissors. Handing it over to Mahesh, who stood panting and quavering by my side, Freddie said: 'You are the resident barber of this place. Now, crop his hair short!'

Overwrought, as Mahesh started clipping my hair, Freddie interjected, 'Don't try making him a movie hero! Look, just clear off the top patch from his pate. Let the rest remain like a historical monument!'

In Mahesh's gaze that fell on me, I could discern both misery and sympathy. Fearing the consequences of disobedience, he started using the scissors. Like a forested hill being cleared on one side, when my scalp was exposed, Freddie Robert gave permission to stop the trimming. I felt a heat only on the part of the skull bereft of hair.

'We are familiar with Brahmins with a knot on their crown, right? Here is a modern Brahmin with his crown shaved off!'

Freddie and his acolytes laughed uproariously.

'I have a secularistic idea, Chitragupta. Look at the harvest on his chest! Hair is an unnecessary object, isn't it? Get me a razor, fast!'

'Is there shaving, apart from cutting?'

'For Brahmins, cleanliness and hairlessness are both equally important!'

I was extremely distressed when Chitragupta arrived with a razor.

'Bhima, don't move!'

Holding the razor against my torso, Freddie Robert drew a vertical line straight down. Then another horizontally. A cross appeared on my chest. If I had felt hot where the hair was cleared, I felt cold where the cross emerged.

'You, Brahmin without the knot on your crown, carrying a cross on your chest, drape yourself with the mundu and proceed to your room. Then read the seventh canto of Shrimad Bhagavad and the eighth chapter of Mark's Gospel one after the other.'

Dragging my body, drained in mortification and terror, with the helplessness of the Cross-Bearer, I walked along with the other three. Their heads displayed spots of wastelands too. They had escaped carrying the cross since they didn't have a hirsute chest like mine.

I could not continue in that hell anymore. A higher education built on suffering was anathema to me. On reaching the room, I decided to head home with the vitiligo-affected bag. One could survive, as could my parents and younger ones, by selling papads or sweetmeats.

Although my roommates tried to dissuade me in various ways, I refused to succumb. I did not yield to their advice, which included, 'You can cover the cross with your shirt', 'The hair on your crown will grow back in a week', 'Don't spoil your future . . .' Without thinking of the dangers of stepping out into the night, I crossed the steps with my bag.

As if receiving the punishment for my defiance, I ended up before the savage gang.

'Bhimasena, you false Brahmin, trying to escape, are you?'

Someone had me in a chokehold. Blowing smoke into my face from the cigarette burning in his lips, Freddie entrapped me inside the 'smokescreen'.

'Well, you can start for home tomorrow after the circumcision ceremony tonight!'

I was hearing the word 'circumcision' for the first time. As soon I returned to the room, I enquired about its meaning from my roommates.

'Allah!' Muhammad Rafi gasped. 'That's our rite of cutting the foreskin!'

'Dear God,' I cried, 'my knot has been hacked off. I have a cross on my chest. Now add this Muslim rite to it . . . then?'

'An *All Religions Meeting* on your body!'

Rafi's words and the way he said it provoked laughter even in those adverse circumstances. He also found another defence for his body.

'Lucky that I already underwent a circumcision once! Now they cannot do anything to me.'

Freddie and his gang entered the room and heard his words.

'But what if we *aren't* particular that *only* the foreskin should be cut off? Umm, all of you, buck up and walk to the ground!'

Inadvertently, Muhammad Rafi's hands extended to his pelvis and created a shield.

The grounds below, hewn out of a hillock, had no steps leading down to it. Since all the lights, including those of the hostel, were switched off, everything discernible was concealed. Crickets, as well as an anonymous bird, were the only creatures that produced inauspicious sounds.

Instead of letting us move together, we were sent to the ground one by one. The desolation in the darkness sufficed to reduce half of one's life! While edging forward with the remaining half, a potful of water fell from the skies and hit the head hard. It took a few moments to realize that the deluge had not originated from the sky; instead, had been propelled from the hostel's water tank. The force of each bucket of water flung from the third-storey terrace had the impact of a rock.

Since it was an unexpected air assault in the darkness, momentarily, the dilemma was which was the greater danger—water or land. If one panicked and rushed into the darkness ahead, it was a sheer fall from the heights to the grounds below. Most would be half-dead in that free fall over two metres.

When I remembered that they were going to try the harsh police-like 'third degree treatment' in the grounds, I had a foreboding that it could turn out to be my last night. A recent piece of news that I had read about a student's death due to cruel ragging terrified me further. I was in a concentration camp beyond the arms of the law.

Anticipating death in the darkness ahead, almost sure of it, as I moved towards the grounds, an arm established its authority on the back of my neck.

'Walk on!'

With that clasp around the neck, I was ushered to the back of the hostel instead of the ground. It guided me through a side door into the hostel, and I was locked inside the darkness of a room.

Shortly, a light was switched on.

Freddie Robert!

I reflected that the bundles of the sins caused by my past life karmas had not yet relinquished me. Tomorrow, I might be reduced to a mere news item.

What was he up to now?

'Don't wonder about it. You will not be able to survive what's planned on the grounds tonight. Think of it like this—I saved you. Three more shall follow soon.'

I was inclined not to believe it.

What was a sadist, who enjoyed torturing, to gain by saving me?

This was another one of his masquerades!

Not pausing to address my incredulity, Freddie Robert left after switching off the light. He did not forget to warn me against using the light.

I attempted to reach the door in that pitch darkness.

It was latched from outside.

As I sat staring into the dark uncertainty in that room, the sound of someone at the door provoked sheer terror in me.

Not one or two, but a horde came into the Stygian darkness. Darkness was an ideal environment for devils.

6

SAHADEVA

From Kuttanadu, I had to hitch a boat ride to join the group going in search of Freddie.

I am Sahadeva.

The last born among the Pandavas.

Someone who eventually forgot his real name of Sudhakaran. One who totally surrendered to the mesmerizing beauty and waterways of Kuttanadu, where he was born.

Nature gave me the colour of Kuttanadu's clay and slush. That colour, which I inherited as my legacy from parents who toiled in the farms and mud, secured me a nickname in the hostel—'Iruttu', alias 'darkness'.

It was warranted not just because there were no hierarchies between darkness and me when it came to skin colour, but also because of my endeavours to constantly keep my hostel room dark.

I had become addicted to that perverse pleasure right from my childhood. By shutting the windows and doors of a room, I always attempted to perfect its solitude.

Truly, I am unaware how my mental state became so dark. As far as I am concerned, this is the normal state of affairs with nothing incongruous about it. Fighting and defeating every ray of light which yearned to creep through the crevices of the windows was my favourite pastime. By stuffing the gaps with black paper, I combated the spread of light. My residence turned into an unvanquished fortress of darkness.

I experienced the accumulation of potential energy in the stillness and solitariness entailed by the darkness. Storing it like a battery, I could easily convert that into the kinetic energy required for my routine activities. If you tell me that the major source of human energy is food, I shall never accept it.

However, when I was a first-year engineering student, storing and transforming energy became relatively impossible. In a room of four, I couldn't create darkness at will or become reclusive. As a result, I had to skip classes, sneak back into the hostel without my roommates' knowledge and then spar with sunlight by plugging the gaps in the windows. I always carried with me the black varnish paper needed to cover the windowpanes.

Freddie Robert, while forcing me to open my bag during the ragging session, had seen the black varnish papers and smelled something fishy. It was Freddie again who discovered my love of darkness after anointing me as Sahadeva and making me a member of the Pandava fellowship. By that time, both of us were in the same class.

In retrospect, I can see that it was the unnatural blending of many coincidences. Else, how would a senior student who ragged us sadistically end up as our group leader and classmate?

Leaving behind our trips and get-togethers, he went searching for some truth of the forest.

Unlike the rest, I find nothing aberrant in that. I understand the peregrinations of his mind more than anyone else. If the truth of the forest touched him like the verity of darkness has touched me, I cannot view it as 'losing the way'. It is normal for someone's natural proclivity to be regarded as unnatural by another.

Freddie might have been received warmly by some cave in the forest. When I reach the mouth of that cave, crossing through the forest, I shall be able to sense his presence. Entering the cave that holds him, I shall recognize my friend Freddie Robert in that darkness.

Recognition, that alone is friendship.

7

PANCHALI

'What a strange name—Panchali!'

I had once raised the query to Freddie Robert.

'Why, Meera? Haven't you familiarized yourself with that name yet? Let's supplant it with Draupadi then! The one who moves fast . . . Druda-pada—what about that?'

'How many interpretations for each word! See, my schooling was in Bengaluru. There wasn't anyone there to tell me tales of the Pandavas or Panchali. Agatha Christie's books and Perry Mason novels were my favourites. Oh, the thrill of reading those! I can relive the feeling when I become Panchali in this Pandava fellowship. That's why I decided to join the gang.'

'If so, on getting to know the reality of Panchali, you might change your decision.'

'Wait, you mean to imply that she slept with the five Pandavas?'

'If yes, then?'

'Take it that this Panchali is ready too! But I have certain conditions. The first Pandava should not budge an inch from truth and dharma. Ready?'

'No way! Except for the name, you shall never be allowed to be Panchali in action. A sort of joke, till all six disperse in their own ways. That's all.'

'But not for me, Freddie. In my case, what's life for you is a joke and what's a joke for you becomes life. Every day which trails to its end in the college is depriving me of something precious.'

As if I had thrown an ice cube straight into his mind, I could poignantly sense the coolness spread through Freddie. If he was a glass of an intoxicating drink, I claim my stake on half of it.

Yet I knew that never would I fall in love with either Freddie or the rest of the Pandavas. Not an inappropriate word or a misdeed ever came from any of them. Though I did not don it, the role of Panchali was to be actualized by me alone. It was akin to the periods which arrived precisely with the lunar month; very natural, yet an intensely private affair. But it was not the temporary protection of a sanitary pad which could be discarded easily that I sought from that pretence. I needed to know exactly what Panchali was and how she would be fulfilled.

There was only one person who could come to my aid in that path. The native of Chalakudy, Aravindan, who balanced himself equably on two fronts: poetry and teaching. Aravindan had more than a student-mentor relationship with Freddie. He would not think twice before snagging the cigarette from his student's lips or bringing the half-finished bottle of liquor close to his own. Beyond all that, his inner world was slippery and lubricious.

Probably due to that, he turned engineering classes into poems of rhyme and metre. He was simple enough to indulge the friendly arm of a student slipping across his shoulders.

I knew that Aravindan was madly in love with me and also that he would never reveal it. Hence, I never mulled about my response in case he made a proposal of love. An incorrect belief, that a denizen of Chalakudy would never open his heart, had taken hold of me. But now I feel that I really liked Aravindan.

But love, strangely enough, never appeared in my path to display its peacock feathers. And peacocks which do not flutter their tails are not worthy of love, let alone an hour of passion! I arrived at a natural conclusion about Aravindan. He was the sort who would decide on a romantic whim upon waking up, to commit suicide.

My conclusion had the precision of a prophecy.

The man removed his body, like an unsuitable raiment, and the secret behind it remained incomprehensible to both teachers and students. He hanged himself, exposing his soul, on the edges of the rice field behind the ladies' hostel.

Everybody except Freddie Robert arrived to catch a glimpse of that romantic end. One isn't sure why he didn't come: a lack of courage to witness that scene or possessing the audacity to overcome death?

Wondering what Aravindan was shouting out to the world in that state, I endured an existence without answers for a long time.

Even if one tried to understand death and suicide to some extent, the fact that a valued teacher of engineering lay dangling in the nakedness of his soul, mocking the world, implied what?

It was a psychological distance I could never gauge with ordinary measuring instruments. Suicide, it seems, does not require even the flimsiest of reasons nowadays!

Now that I think about it, there are certain traces of that in Freddie Robert's sudden disappearance too. Like the teacher becoming naked before death, the student turned naked before life. Why is my mind finding something reprehensible in the common factor of 'nakedness' in both? If the body is merely a garment of the soul, on leaving it behind, weren't all souls, including mine, turning naked?

If so, nakedness is not of the body. The body is merely a cover for the nakedness.

It must be the universal mind, extending across ages, which connected Aravindan and Freddie. Notwithstanding the different time spheres, those who were touching it experienced similar thoughts.

I was hardly affected by Aravindan's suicide. Not just me, it impacted nobody in college or anything in the world! It passed away like a drizzle or a breeze occurring in the world on a Tuesday morning. Freddie Robert's disappearance was also supposed to be like that. But, owing to my inability to accept it as a matter of course, the incident affected me in many ways.

When one of the five elements departs, it definitely impacts whatever it was which linked the five together. In the place of the *full stop* left behind by Aravindan, Freddie had left behind a *semicolon*.

Semicolons are always troublesome. And dangerous.

That was how I was forced to return, again and again, to the interpretations Aravindan had revealed. He had elucidated that Panchali was the mind which spread across the '*panchendriya*', the five senses, and it was the quick movement of the mind which got her the name Draupadi. One could also see her as the life spirit traversing through the '*panchabhoota*': the five elements of earth, sky, fire, water and ether.

'She will always stand with the five essential qualities known as Pandavas. When dharma, strength, originality, personality, and the knowledge of the Vedas come together, the progress which ensues is called Draupadi.'

On hearing me parrot what Aravindan had told me, Freddie burst into laughter and asked:

'So shall Draupadi come along when these five qualities leave for their forest stint?'

I did not feel obliged to answer that question then. Neither did I consider that I would have to answer a question through my actions. And consider what happened!

Panchali, known as Draupadi, was now raring for her forest stint!

I have come to experience that, mostly, words spoken unthinkingly come true in the future.

I am sure that in this forest trip I shall discover Freddie Robert. Panchali is travelling today on the train to the city, to wipe away the semicolon and establish a full stop in its place. Towards the forest which had sucked in Freddie Robert with the extreme density of a black hole.

8

REUNION

After travelling diverse paths, when we got together in the city, it seemed like meeting one another after ages. Hardly a month had passed since the final examinations, when we had dispersed. Still, it felt as if many years of separation had created a distance between us. Each of us was silent inwardly, unable to even greet another. What was left to share when we knew it all?

Two differences marked the impending journey.

One, Meera's presence.

Two, Freddie Robert's absence.

Often, we were prevented from taking Meera along due to the limitations imposed by the feminine physique. But Meera always insisted on accompanying us on our forest trips. She fought with Freddie on her exclusion.

'Man's progress is only in speech! You all are very narrow-minded, those who assume that women can never match up to men.'

'It's not that, Meera,' Freddie protested. 'The journey to the forest is fraught with many dangers. Each has to take care of himself.'

'Ah, I shall take care of my own self! What is the relevance of a *vanavasa* for the Pandavas, without Panchali?'

'See, you and I can conclude that. But our society does not permit a woman a secret trip to the forest with five men.'

'Did you have society's written sanction before allowing me into your group? Or did I have one before I joined? Freddie, this is sheer hypocrisy! If you don't take me along on the next trip, rewrite the story of the Mahaprasthana—the last great journey of the Pandavas—by mentioning that Panchali reached heaven first!'

Such bargaining and arguments elevated Meera to a co-traveller in the small expeditions which followed soon after. But she could never visit Pullothikkadu. Owing to her uncle's death, she could not accompany us on our last trip with Freddie Robert. And that journey, incomplete without Panchali, had ended disastrously.

Some new travel rules were being created among us on this new trip with Meera. Perhaps Meera could grasp the passion Freddie had for nature. Rather, we hoped that Meera herself would attract Freddie like a magnet from the forests!

We had to travel by bus to the valley from the town. The less-than-normal-sized bus had fewer seats than usual. It was difficult for bigger buses to travel through the rugged terrain, which was undulating and full of hairpin curves.

Most of the travellers belonged to the lower strata of society. With faces shadowed by woes, holding many bundles and vegetable baskets, they huddled on the seats and available spaces. Most were returning from the town after selling their wares: vegetables, wild honey, fragrant spices and other curiosities of the forest. Women with lips reddened by betel leaves and eyes lined with kohl; men with golden-brown hair and brawny muscles. Their hutments lay scattered around the valley.

During the journey, all the co-travellers watched us with interest. It was clear that Meera, clad in jeans and shirt, was the focus of their attention. They chattered about it in their tribal language. Meera seemed to be discomfited that she was the cynosure of all eyes.

Mahesh spoke, to create a diversion: 'How did you manage to get away from home, Meera?'

'The most convenient fib in today's circumstances: a job interview!'

'What if we are delayed by a few days? Won't they start searching?'

'Since dad is busy establishing his new business empire, he won't be any trouble. That leaves mom, who has forgotten about her daughter! I am a free bird, and my sky is unlimited. Now I quite understand Freddie's intuitions.'

'Meera, what are you speaking of?'

'Hey, was wondering why none of us ever understood him. Though we were close to him, we were never his true friends, were we?'

It was Muhammad Rafi who replied to that.

'He never disclosed anything about himself. But he always remembered every single detail about us!'

'Where did he get all that money from? As if he was some sort of a landlord's son?'

'He was a landlord's son! A real gold mine. He mocked himself by saying he was from Kalgoorlie and Coolgardie, the Australian towns known for the gold rush!'

'But of one thing I'm sure,' Sahadeva Iyer interrupted, 'his mind was as rich as a gold mine! If Freddie wasn't there to help me, I would have dropped out long ago and returned to selling papads. He helped me without letting anyone know. My calculator, books, even my fees were paid for only because of him!'

The others gazed compassionately as the Bhimasena inside that bulky body started melting. His voice was trembling.

Sudhakaran, shedding his usual reticence, joined in then.

'There is something worrying me.'

'What?'

'Did the flow of money stop towards the end? He was pretending nothing was amiss.'

'Why do you think so?' Meera enquired.

'Lots of factors. That profligacy of his was gone much before he went back to nature. He cut down on the usual parties and expensive trips. As if he was forced to step down from whatever he once was . . .'

'But he never told us anything!'

'That he did not shows his authenticity. His hand was used only to giving, not taking. And we, we just shamelessly kept on taking! Never giving back even a percentage of it.'

That was the truth.

Freddie always came up with reasons for celebration. Through him, we became familiar with rich food and expensive drinks. Though we were heavily indebted to him, never did it strike us to organize a small party for him. In those feasts that he threw, without counting costs, we simply walked in, hands swinging, like beggars.

'You Pandavas ought to be ashamed of yourselves,' Meera accused, 'sticking with Freddie in order to get everything and never coming to *realize* what he truly was!'

We deserved that accusation. But we had never expected to face such a situation when interacting closely with him. How

Freddie tried to hide his own self sometimes became clear to us much later, like a point of sanity between bouts of madness.

What was he running away from?

Or whom?

We failed to find an estuary that would enable a direct entry into his mind. Instead, we sailed across continents, never reaching him, and anchored on foreign shores.

'If we knew his real problem . . .?' Meera stopped midway.

'And if we did?'

'Who knows if we wouldn't escape into the forests too?'

Our bus kept travelling through the ups and downs of the earth. Soon, in the distance, we could catch glimpses of the forest. There was a stream on the left, running parallel to the road. A stream full of fresh, cool water, originating in the forest.

We saw hordes arriving in private vehicles, playing in the water. On display was an alacrity to shrug off the city, which they had left behind.

Beyond the stream was a dense bamboo jungle. Then there were mangroves. And further on, as we saw the gigantic trees raising their heads, we recollected the shlokas from the Vrikshayurveda, the treatise on trees, from which Freddie used to quote often. Owing to our lack of proficiency in Sanskrit, we could not learn the lines by heart, yet the concepts penetrated deep.

Equivalent of ten wells, one pond.

Equivalent of ten ponds, one lake.

Equivalent of ten lakes, a son.

Equivalent of ten sons, a tree.

What, then, was so surprising about the fact that after realizing the existence of an incomparable great forest full of gigantic trees, Freddie Robert's centre of gravity stayed rooted in it?

As we edged closer to the valley, signs of human settlement became scarce. Occasionally, there were a few thatched huts, scraggly cattle, domesticated birds . . . Inside the bus, besides us, very few passengers remained.

One could see the mountain ranges, like pyramids, at a distance. When sunlight fell on the mist-covered mountains, they sparkled like blue volcanoes. Pointing at a peak, which stood apart from the rest, Sahadeva Iyer cried: 'Look, Pullothikkadu!'

Meera's heart leapt on hearing the forest's name. Peeping out of the window, she glanced in the direction that Iyer was pointing at. The formidable forest which hid humans! From a distance, it looked like a blue sketch of a mountain. A straight line drawn to it would comprise many miles.

The bus stopped in the valley, sputtering and heaving and exhibiting all its travel fatigue. It had grown tired due to its old age. Throughout the way, it had displayed the breathing troubles of a chronic asthma patient. A few tribals ended their journey along with us. Some shacks and a tea shop were the only conveniences in the place.

By the wayside was a century-old raised stone. Beneath that stone-rest, where many headloads had been placed by travellers of yore, two bovines were resting comfortably, ignoring everyone. Another cow, standing, observed us attentively. In its still pose, it looked like the statue of a cow bearing a stone-rest!

The only refuge was a guest house owned by the Forest Department. Since we showered the watchman Maniyan with Scotch whisky whenever we visited the forest, he usually made all the arrangements for our stay. The only prerequisite was that none of the top shots of the department should be around for their jaunts during that time! For that nosey parker Maniyan, who believed that all civilized men turned savage behind shut doors, our visits were an aberration. Seeing Meera in the gang, his doubts were stirred. Smelling a lecherous game afoot, he looked askance at us. Probably the worst possibility he must have visualized was a gang molestation.

We told Maniyan the truth of our journey, showing him the news cutting about Freddie Robert. He told us that the environmental researchers who had visited the forest in the previous week had 'rested' in the same guest house. In recent times, nobody else but them had ventured into the forests. Maybe an odd Kani tribal might have strayed inside to collect wild honey. The watchman expressed his astonishment at Freddie surviving in a deep forest full of wild animals.

Maniyan made arrangements for us to spend the night. Instead of opting for a separate room, Meera preferred to stay with us. Hearing that, Muhammad Rafi quipped: 'If someone who is unaware of our trip's truth raids this place, the five of us will end up as a salacious news item tomorrow!'

'Entering the forest without permission is also against the law,' Maniyan interjected slyly.

'Doesn't matter, we are trailing someone who disregarded all laws. See, laws affect only those bound by them. If I am a Pakistani, irrespective of where I am, I shall be bound by the laws of my country! For someone, who in his mind, crosses all boundaries of nations and even those of the universe, no laws apply. These are not my words, but Freddie's.'

As soon as he heard that the usual drinking spree wouldn't happen this time, Maniyan's enthusiasm dwindled. That problem was solved by handing over a hefty amount for his use. Maniyan's torch moved away, casting patches of light en route to the place where money morphed into liquor.

'Tomorrow we have a tough climb. Let us rest properly.' With that comment, Mahesh sought out the cot.

Then Meera asked: 'You said Freddie's diary was with you. I need it for some time.'

'Right now?'

'I am determined to finish it tonight. What if we find a road sign in it that leads to him?'

'I found nothing after reading it. But that doesn't mean that a woman won't be able find something a man couldn't! Let us have a woman's reading now.'

Opening his bag, Mahesh retrieved a diary clad in brown plastic and gave it to Meera. After dinner, when the others surrendered to sleep under thick woollen blankets, Meera opened the diary.

A yellow-coloured insect lay stuffed inside the page she opened. She blew away the remnants of that hexapod and started reading.

It was a night from some ghostly tale.

9

BHIKSHAM DEHI

I met that strange man at a halting place during a forest trip.

'Halting place' is perhaps the wrong word.

How can a dark cave in the midst of desolate mountains be termed as one?

I had eight hours' worth of walking before I could return. A beautiful bird unsighted before in either ornithological expeditions or books! Its movement went against the typical flying style of a bird. Hiding behind the bushes, trying to capture an image in my camera, I followed it for a long distance, losing my way.

What if it was arduous? Freddie Robert was going to present to the world a bird never before identified! Meanwhile, I had crossed into the unknown frontiers of the forest. A person with single-minded focus becomes oblivious of the environment, and I was as such, questing after the bird, forgetting myself.

Whenever I was on the verge of capturing it, it would fly off. The creature was mesmerizing, and I couldn't help following it. And then, after making me travel quite a distance with its game of hide and seek, it pirouetted for a pose in front of my camera. By then, the sun was setting. Fearing that wild animals would soon step out in the night, I was hurrying back when I met the mendicant.

'No more travel today, my child,' the old man forbade me.

His long beard trailed downwards beyond the chest. A penetrating look darted from between greying eyebrows. Deepening the gaze was some sort of sandalwood paste slathered over the 'third eye' on his forehead. A soiled piece of clothing covered his body.

I was caught in a dilemma. It would be foolish to spend the night with a person whose whereabouts and identity I didn't know. This is an age in which charismatic masters turn out to be frauds. Indeed, nowadays, the devil reads the scriptures seated on commercialized spiritual pedestals.

The old man smiled serenely at my doubtful face. His teeth, untouched by time, shone white. His muscular frame bespoke strength. In a wrestling match, this old man would defeat my youthful self.

'Why expect a robber or a murderer inside the forest?' he questioned me.

Pretending as if I had never had the thought, I glibly commented, 'I forgot the time, being on the mountaintop.'

'That's the specialty of this mountain! If you are at its pinnacle, you feel there is much time before darkness falls. The change occurs in a jiffy. Child, don't travel tonight. There is no light here. Not even a hut nearby.'

'How come you are here all by yourself?' I asked falteringly.

There was no need for an old man to be solitary in the forest unless he was lost like me.

'If someone prefers being alone, he shall be alone. Those who resist being alone, death shall make them alone.' Smiling openly, he gazed at the sky. 'With Amma always present, how can one be alone?'

'Won't the animals be troublesome at night?'

'Child, there are fewer wicked animals in the forest when compared to the mainland. Besides, every forest would have kept aside one place where animals cannot reach. Come, follow me.'

As I accompanied him to the place kept aside by the forest, I enquired: 'Who are you?'

Another smile.

'That is a question which I ask myself. I don't have an answer. Well, if you insist, you can call me Bhiksham Dehi.'

Bhiksham Dehi—a mendicant.

What sort of a name was that?

Bhiksham Dehi made me walk towards the nearby mountain. One had to descend a sheer drop with much difficulty before ascending the next slope.

Roots, which nature conjured to prevent one from slipping! Stepping on those to climb down, we were nearly circumambulating the mountain. It took me to that wondrous sight.

As if a pyramid had been split in the middle, that half of the mountain looked vertical. From the front, the cleaved half was not discernible and consequently, it looked like any other mountain. I was stepping inside a realm transcending what the eyes could see.

I told my mind, and it in turn told me, that this mountain was concealing many things. To climb that cliff, one had to claw at and step on small rocky ledges. The effortless way in which Bhiksham Dehi made his way up filled me with much envy.

'Come, climb up, child!'

Like a toddler stepping cautiously, I started the mountaineering. It was like scaling a huge wall. A little carelessness could make one lose the grip, leading to a headlong fall.

'Don't think of it as a sheer drop. When you ascend, resist looking down. Then you can reach the top without any trouble,' Bhiksham Dehi spoke. 'That means, instead of the past or the future, exist in the present.'

Knowing that contemplating the precipice or looking down would invite danger, I made sure to stay away from both. Immediately both thought and sight started heckling me. Somehow, I followed Bhiksham Dehi up the cliff and then saw the breach inside the mountain.

It was a den. Something invisible from below.

One could squeeze inside and sit without hitting the head. If needed, even stretch oneself.

Again, I told my mind, and it in turn whispered back, that this mountain was concealing many things. The wild animals in the 'nether world' could not reach the den on the summit. A safe haven, which nature had tucked away inside the forest. I could never have imagined such a thing had I not witnessed it myself.

This mountain seemed to be the very heart of the forest. And the man who discovered it was far from ordinary!

'Tonight, you shall be safe here,' Bhiksham Dehi said.

Soon, the forest became dark.

When the fireflies lit the twilight lamps, many prayerful creatures started raising hymns from their own hideaways.

I was above the forest now.

All the forest paths that I had traversed were down below, dim like the past. With the impassivity of one who had conquered the peak, I sat staring at my past. It was like casting a glance at the sea from the top of the lighthouse.

'There, look!'

I looked where Bhiksham Dehi pointed. At a long distance away, I could see dots of lights in the hundreds!

'For Amma, it is the night of lamps. And blessed are the eyes that can watch that from here. You cannot catch this sight from anywhere else. This is Amma's place of origin. Her eyes watch over this place.'

It looked as if it was a temple, clad in the ceremonial dress of lamps aflame at twilight. I wondered why this man was glorifying a sight which could have been easily seen at close quarters.

'There, you can see only the thronging crowds. Here, in peaceful nature, dwells Amma.'

Though Bhiksham Dehi spoke as if he read my mind, I liked that perspective of discovering Amma in nature.

Towards the right of the den, water droplets oozed out of a rock and trickled into an earthen pot; overflowing, it turned into a rivulet, then a stream, joined by many more watercourses, forming into a divine river. It was the stream that I had seen from the bus. On following it, one would reach the sea. That meant, when I touched the water drop, I was touching the sea!

I touched the water. Through it, the sea.

Exquisitely cool water.

As clear as crystal.

Taking a handful of water, I splashed it on my face. Like dew drops, they stuck to me. Much above sea level, with temperatures lower than in the plains, it was getting cold. But it was a pleasant coolness.

'How should I address you? Swami or Guru?' I queried.

That same smile as an answer.

'Who is the guru, who is the disciple? My type is merely the dust on Amma's feet. If necessary, call me Bhiksham Dehi.

But you won't need to, except while thinking of me. Think about it: is there a difference whether the name is Bhiksham Dehi, a dinosaur or a donkey? I am a simple beggar. Are you embarrassed to spend time with such a person?'

'No,' I tried to hide my inner thoughts.

'Child, you too must have a name?'

'Freddie Robert.'

'Aha! Sounds like a fried papad!'

Though I was hearing that a fried papad was hiding inside my name for the first time, I felt it was right.

'By name, Christian. By form, human. What if we remove the name and form?' The mendicant laughed to himself. I disliked that laughter, seemingly of a madman, a guffaw which removed both names and forms. But his words bruised my mind. After deletion of name and form, what remained of a human being?

'Why did you come here? Usually no one ends up here.'

I did not disclose that it was my penchant to end up in places where nobody ventured. Instead, I said this: 'Since I am interested in ornithology, I set off to see the forest. I came here following a stunning bird. It made me walk a long distance!'

'Saw a good bird! And reached a logical end. Ever saw that bird in any of your ornithology texts?'

'No, never. Neither in books nor on websites. I have taken a photograph to discuss it with other birdwatchers.'

'Well, I shall tell you what will happen when you discuss it. The glory of having discovered an unknown bird shall be yours. Perhaps even an epithet of "Freddie Bird" shall be bestowed!'

'Freddie Bird!' I muttered. Something I had forgotten suddenly rekindled in my memory. How many times must I have mentioned to my friends about a bird which kept beckoning me from the forests of the Sahyadri mountains? Was that the one going to be famed as the Freddie Bird? I felt as if two wings were sprouting from both sides of my body and that I was about to lay an egg. Before I could ejaculate it, Bhiksham Dehi continued: 'You are at a spot where there are footprints of the holy one whom death never touches. Child, I see that you are blessed with a rare fortune!'

How could a wastrel, who begged and loitered in the forest, unable to face the world, comprehend that I had only contempt for myself when it came to the fortunes I was blessed with? I have always loathed fortune-tellers.

'Anyway, it is madness to meander alone in the forest. It's a dangerous place and you are alone. There are leopards and tigers here. Death lies waiting in such places, right?'

'I could ask you the same question.'

'What if I live or die? But yours is a different matter, child.'

I am a habitual colonizer of obstinacies. One made its entry and transformed into a conceit about my intrepidity.

'Well, I think otherwise,' I replied haughtily. 'If needed, I can even wrestle with death.'

Bhiksham Dehi laughed loudly enough to annoy me.

'Yes, I have heard about Nachiketas in the puranas . . . Amma, bestow true intelligence on this child.'

This is what I, Freddie Robert, find unacceptable. If I set out on a perverse path, I would like to be ahead. If it is a noble venture, then I want to be at the pinnacle. Freddie shall never be satisfied being an also-ran, and insists on being first. I found the respect I had felt for the mendicant reducing. It was my mistake that I took him for a wise, learned man. He was an imbecile who had never accessed the various interpretations of life. A common turncoat with long beard and hair. I have always detested such folk. Freddie shall never chance his life on anything obscure. And if it were crystal-clear, he would put his life at stake and jump into it.

'Aren't you hungry, child? Don't you want to eat something?' Bhiksham Dehi asked.

Though I was famished, I did not admit it due to my pride. To eat the alms this beggar accumulated would be despicable, sinful.

The last biscuit packet was long finished. A night without food was not a monstrous issue.

'I have some rice, so I will make some rice gruel,' Bhiksham Dehi spoke. 'By adding a couple of red chillies, a slice of onion and salt, it will become a terrific dinner. But the only vessel I have is my begging bowl. Child, will you be able to eat from it?'

I almost threw up on hearing his words.

It was evident that this beggar lacked any semblance of culture. Rather than share food from his begging bowl, it was better to die hungry. He was promising rice gruel made from alms to Freddie Robert, who had played with riches all his life!

Though I was infuriated, considering the situation in the forest, I did not display any feeling.

'I don't want anything. Not hungry at all.'

The same smile at my open rebellion. I disliked that mysterious smile which indicated that he recognized my lie.

In a corner of that den were three stones that formed a makeshift cooking alcove. Placing a pot full of water over the stones, Bhiksham Dehi kindled the fire. I watched with detachment when he retrieved, from his soiled bundle, three fistfuls of rice obtained as alms, and dropped those into the cooking pot.

I diverted my attention to the festival of lights outside. As the darkness intensified, so did the brightness of the flames. It was like a galaxy of lights below. I was like a traveller in the air, watching the earth's night. Tomorrow, after walking eight hours, I would have to anchor myself in that place.

As I watched, a cloud hid the lights. And then it moved, becoming clear again. Along with that, the fragrance of rice boiling in the pot filled the den. By the light of the fire, Bhiksham Dehi's visage was radiant. Or maybe it was just my imagination, owing to the all-encompassing darkness.

Adding chillies, onion and salt to the boiling rice gruel, Bhiksham Dehi created something I had never seen before.

I felt a revulsion on seeing it. As I hoped that he would not coax me to share the food, he poured the hot gruel into his begging bowl, and adding two leaf-spoons to it, invited me to eat.

'The body will curse you if forced to go hungry. Come, we can eat together from this bowl.'

My ego prohibited me from partaking the food. However, my tongue rebelled when my insides started burning with hunger. It was as if all the hunger experienced till date had returned altogether to their origin.

The stomach was the sacrificial pyre.

Sparking from the holy flintstone blazed the *jadaragni*, fire of the stomach.

The pyre was thirsting for the sacrificial offering, and when it became overwhelming, in the blazing hunger, my ego's first outer shell was shed.

When I picked up the leaf-spoon to share alms from the beggar's bowl, I realized that on the verge of dying from starvation, even a millionaire would wrestle with street dogs for leftovers.

What shall I call myself, the one who had received alms from Bhiksham Dehi?

Whatever that maybe, today, I have eaten the tastiest food life has ever offered.

10

THE CALLING

Night.

A cloud covered the face of the den, and shoved its way inside. In that obscurity, so dense as to touch the body, the vision of lights vanished completely.

I checked the time in my watch with its radium dial. Seeing that its hands were still, like those of a hanged person, I was perplexed. The watch, which had been loyal to a fault till now, always exact, had now failed to keep time.

The Lord of Time, having stopped moving, seemed to have slipped into deep sleep on the mountaintop.

I became aware of a creeping fear.

Who was this bearded mendicant?

What was his goal?

One cloth bag and sufficient money were in my possession. There was no guarantee that he wouldn't finish me off in the heart of the forest and steal the goods.

I recollected seeing a billhook in the faint light inside the den. Planning to use it if the circumstances so arose, I tried to estimate the location in the darkness. As my hands searched over the rugged rock and tightened its grip on the scythe, Bhiksham Dehi's sigh arose, 'Amma!' When I hurriedly tried to stuff the weapon below my cloth bag, the sharp edge knocked hard against my left arm.

'Amma,' I cried out too, unthinkingly.

'What's up, child?' Bhiksham Dehi called. 'Saw something scary?'

I covered the cut on my left arm with my right hand. It was not deep enough to bleed profusely. Rather than a gory gash, the wound was like a mild warning. My timid mind whispered that it was punishment for suspecting the mendicant. But the other half of my mind, sceptical of omens, locked horns with it.

All those mutinous thoughts kidnapped my sleep and started negotiating the costs.

Reclining on the rock called for much vigilance. If one rolled over unwittingly, it would be a sheer drop down the den. There was evidence of animals prowling in that space. It could be a wild creature which had sniffed human blood. Or it might be the dinner chatter of the wild rats that came to nibble the food thrown by the mendicant.

Creating a pillow out of my left hand, I had carefully turned on my side when I heard a musical instrument.

Percussion instruments of a temple?

Astounded at the music in the middle of the forest, I listened carefully. Could I be hearing the wild music beats of savages?

No, nothing.

When I shrugged it off as a vignette of my imagination and lay down to sleep, the tune repeated itself.

From where did it originate?

Now it was very clear to me that the sound had not descended from the air. Gripped by doubt, I listened with my left ear close to the rock.

My hair stood on end at the moment when the barrier between the ear and the smooth rock disappeared.

From the depths of the rock, the beat of Shiva's drum was gushing towards me. The music of nature's first phase.

Doubting my hearing, I raised my head and listened intently, experimenting multiple times.

Takdam takidakida, takidakida, takidakida,
Takidam takidakida, takidakida, takidakida . . .

Truly *Rudra taal*, the drum beat of Shiva!

In that timeless flow of rhythm, my eyes streamed with tears. My inner ears became alert to the universe's drumbeats. A state where the material world of man and nature disappears and turns into just a vibration. The level of existence where one becomes many, and many becomes one.

In the same instant, the mist moved away from the den and the fiesta of lights at Amma's home flamed high.

'Amma,' both Bhiksham Dehi and I enunciated in harmony.

When the two cries intermingled and started off on a journey from the middle of the forest, sitting cross-legged on the ground inside the den, with the haplessness of a lost child, forgetting myself, I folded my hands towards Amma at the distance.

Amma.

Mother of Mourning and Eternal Succour.

Here I was, riding Amma's chest, amid the omnipresent skies.

I, Freddie Robert, recognize at this moment that there is only 'One Mother' for the entire world. He knows that it is not

'I' who guard 'myself' inside the forest, but 'Mother Nature', who waited with a den ready inside a steep cliff.

I would not have been welcomed as a guest in this night retreat, except for the purpose of attaining Amma. Instead of my Amma in the mortal world, who was separated from me even before the umbilical cord broke off, I was getting an Amma for eternity. How ineffectual was this 'body' named Freddie Robert, the denizen of a den in the forest depths!

I am at the centre point of the universe now. The centre point which was the basis for the crores and crores of galaxies containing the sun, moon and stars.

Here begins the heartbeat of time.

From the first movement, dividing into Accretion-Diminution, the duality of the universe originates.

Slowly, I laid myself down.

Onto the rock. The rock which was both my roof and my foundation.

In the secret of the nature where the roof and foundation mutually transformed into each other, utterly fearless, I lay like a child in the lap of his mother.

The rhythm of the water-clock which dripped into the mud pot as a great river rocked me to a serene sleep.

In the morning, when I woke up, Bhiksham Dehi was absent.

Where had he gone?

A ragged woollen blanket was draped around me. The mendicant had yet again given me alms. I did not feel the least distaste for the tattered covering.

Instantly, the night's fierce drumbeat came to me. I listened with my ears against the rock.

No, I could hear nothing.

Doubt washed over me.

I removed the blanket. It was cold enough to freeze one's bone marrow. Everything was encompassed by mists.

Rays of light were scattering in the fog.

With an entrancing beauty, an aerial view of the forest presented itself.

The vast canopy of the trees resembled dense clouds. There was a mélange of morning melodies by myriad birds.

It was a futile effort to discern the distant temple by staring in the direction of the night lamps. There was nothing to be seen in the day! In the night, the splendour of the lights had been revealed to me. Let it stay in my life, marking the fortune of having spent one night in this resting place.

It was time for me to return.

'Amma!'

Bhiksham Dehi's sound could be heard far below.

Perhaps he had returned after the morning ablutions.

'Woke up?' Bhiksham Dehi queried. 'Must have been afraid at night!'

I had many a bundle of enquiries in my custody. Lots indeed, inclusive of the drumbeat throbbing in the rock and the presence which had assumed the form of clouds . . .

I did not seek anything. 'For some questions, there were no answers to be expected from others' came the answer from my own self. Also, that 'The one who receives answers from within, needn't search for answers without.'

'I need to go down the mountain before the sunlight intensifies,' I called out.

'Sure, if you start now, you will be able to catch a bus by two o'clock. Seven hours if you walk fast. There is a stream on the way where you can take a dip. Carry out your ablutions nearby. One and half hours of walking ahead will bring you to a shack. After your bath, eat this fruit; you won't feel tired.'

All my travel instructions were being offered uninterruptedly.

I lifted my bundle.

A simple journey where there was nothing to prepare for.

A humble sojourn where there was no worry about leaving anything behind.

It was gruelling to descend from the den. The ascent had been comparatively easier. Such a steep slope, looking as if a slice of mountain was abruptly chopped off, would be a rare sight in the world. A place made holy by some great soul with silence. And so, I named that Muni Mala, the mountain of the sage who practises silence.

Somehow, I dared to climb down and reach the mendicant. I was drenched from head to toe in the purity of the condensing dewdrops.

'It is better to travel alone,' Bhiksham Dehi commented. 'If there are too many minds, it gets shattered.'

What was he implying?

Suddenly I remembered my Pandava gang. It was true that I had been oblivious of them in the mysterious ambience of the forest. Like someone who stepped down from Turiya to Jagrata—transcendental consciousness to waking consciousness—back to college.

Before that, I mouthed some courteous words.

'Thank you. For providing a refuge in the night!'

'Everything is Amma's benevolence!'

'Shall I leave?'

'Do come back, do come back,' the mendicant said twice.

I would never return to that place. Then why was the blessing showered twice?

An incompleteness within kept elbowing me. Something vague. When I readied to journey back in that confusion, Bhiksham Dehi asked: 'Did you mean it truly yesterday?'

'What?'

'That you are ready to wrestle with death?'

I could not reply with full conviction. Not even with half conviction.

'Child,' Bhiksham Dehi said, 'life and death are not separate but one. The wrestling with death will turn out to be wrestling with life itself.'

After saying that, holding a small bowl, he ascended with total ease towards the den.

For a little while, I stood still, like a man forced into a duel with death.

Not wanting to stay there, I moved towards the stream. I hung my binoculars around my neck, like the memory of a past birth which was of no use any more.

After a while, when I looked back, the den had disappeared from my view.

The unflappable steadiness of the faraway mountain.

Traversing through the wild path which accepted the solitary traveller, as I washed my feet in the rivulet's cold water, a moist truth clambered inside me. I decided to take a dip and absolve myself of all misinformation and misdeeds.

I wept.

Remembering a certain Freddie Robert.

Thinking of something which would continue to stain in spite of that cleansing dip.

Shrugging off the inner burden as resolutely as possible, I emerged light-heartedly from the river and bit into the fruit offered by the mendicant.

Now I had to hurry to the valley and catch the bus.

A moment.

My feet turned back to the original path I had stepped through.

When the feet turn, one's path in life itself changes. Just as in the case of the one who, moving towards death, swerves towards life, it is the feet that determine a man.

Like a puppet pulled by strings, re-determining me, my feet started diminishing the distance I had left behind from the den.

11

WILLPOWER

'Came back, didn't you? I had made a forbidden wish. Please let that child return . . . And Amma replied, yes, I am sending him back!' Bhiksham Dehi murmured with an open smile.

He looked as if he had been waiting for my return. I had not even thought of a reason for coming back. Neither had I any specific plans. It was as if someone else had changed the direction, with a remote control, of the one who had gone in for a dip in the stream.

'It is not the outer part of the bather alone that is purified but the inner too. If one can enjoy that immersion for six days, what great fortune! *"After crossing the six steps, you shall see Him."* Haven't you heard that hymn?'

'Shall I be allowed to stay for six days then?' I asked diffidently.

'Desire means to deserve. Now, what's it that stands in opposition and disturbs you?'

What was troubling me?

Really, was there anything?

Bhiksham Dehi climbed down from the den. Sitting on a rock, he sat me down by his side. When he stared at my face, I felt the embarrassment of a person unravelling the real me, one that I had got used to covering up habitually.

The rock was tenderly warm since the sunshine was growing intense. How come it was smooth as a female belly?

If he was psychic, he would be able to decipher my wayward ruminations. And if he could, he would refuse to accept me.

'The life of a living creature is pathetic,' sighed Bhiksham Dehi. 'When pride clouds the intelligence, what remains is only passion. What's the use of being passionate?'

I couldn't make much sense of that sudden change of direction. As I sat listening silently, he added:

'There is something far beyond all that. Willpower. This forest and the steep mountain cliff exist only due to willpower. Do you have that, child?'

The truth was that I, Freddie Robert, had never thought of it. Yet, I ended up blurting out: 'I think I do have.'

'Just being sure won't do. One needs proof!'

'Go ahead, check.'

My inherent daredevilry, which always challenged everything, hardened further. Meanwhile, digging his finger into a small cavity in the rock, the mendicant unearthed something and placed it on my arm.

'Ahh, Amma!' I screamed at the top of my voice.

'Is this willpower? Someone who cannot endure the bite of a wild ant?' Bhiksham Dehi quipped, brushing away my pride.

The place where the ant bit stung like hell.

It was obviously venomous.

Instantly, my swollen arm turned blue-black. An intolerable, itching pain began. I felt faint. The mad old man had hurt me much.

As I sat flustered and furious, Bhiksham Dehi uprooted a green plant and, crushing its roots, slathered the juice on my arm.

'Even an unanticipated ant bite can be excruciating. Learn to face it with resilience.'

I did not reply. As I contemplated the stupidity of returning for an ant bite, Bhiksham Dehi asked another question.

'The silliest adversity in the forest is an ant bite. If you cannot tolerate even that, you better return to those riches, which you think are beyond any ant's bite, but in fact are prone to destruction, swarmed by ants.'

'No, I am not returning!' I sniped obstinately. 'Try getting me bitten by an ant again if you want!'

It was my obduracy, my own sibling, which made me say that. The obduracy which loathed bowing its head before anyone or anything.

'Let it be so,' Bhiksham Dehi replied.

He caught a comparatively large ant this time. Its size was fearsome. Rotating its poisonous thorny pincers, it was readying to attack the unseen foe. The mendicant was trying to throw me off balance by displaying the ant in all its ferocity. The ant was moving its threatening organs as if in a body-building exhibition. But I was determined that whatever be the experience, I wouldn't be afraid.

This time around, the ant injected its needle in my right arm.

It was more painful than the first experience.

Grinding my teeth and suffocating in my struggle, I forcibly held myself back. The deadly mandibles of the wild ant speared deep inside me.

I sat staring at the unshakeable mountains, holding fast to a willpower that refused to budge before anything, refusing my mind access to my arm. 'The one who becomes an unmoving mountain touches infinite strength,' I realized.

The infinite vistas of stillness.

My arm was covered with a poison-blue hue.

I underwent an experience of the veins accepting the poison and handing it over to the brain, turning it into a feeling of exhilaration. Venom which triggered ecstasy!

'People die due to poisonous bites, unable to handle its exhilaration,' Bhiksham Dehi said. This time around, he did not try any herbal healing. Instead, he offered a piece of wisdom.

'The first lesson is this, my child! Repetition reduces the intensity of an experience. If this is repeated four or five times, you will hardly acknowledge the bite of a wild ant. Even huge animals are killed when these wild ants attack in hordes. Your veins carry its poison now.'

Picking up a harmless ant, Bhiksham Dehi forced it to bite my bluish arm. In seconds, it shivered and died.

'When you are here, I shall test you—whether the vessel I have been searching for is with you.'

'Which vessel?'

'What does a mendicant have but his begging bowl? You should always keep it clean. After all, we don't know who will offer alms at what time! What if it happens to be a rich king? Suppose he is pleased to see the sparkling bowl and fills it till it overflows?'

I couldn't gauge the inner meaning of those words. Could it be that the richest man in the world was a mystical wanderer? Someone who owned the whole world?

Yes. My mind confirmed it strongly.

'Now, Freddie Robert, you rest on this rock.' Bhiksham Dehi took my name for the very first time. 'Let all your senses— your eyes, your ears—rest. Continue like that as long as you can, without your mind getting entangled in anything at all. Become a silent spectator to whatever comes and goes. Let the birds fly in the sky. Let the trees dance on. And let the animals prowl around. You simply watch everything. There won't be anybody for you to talk with out here. But when you are alone, you shall realize that you are talking to everything and that they are responding. In between, your hunger will arise. Let me visit the tribal village on the border to get something to assuage the hunger pangs.'

'Shall I come along?'

'No, it is I who should go!' The mendicant emphasized the word 'I'.

'I shall be all alone here.'

'Is the obstinate fellow's willpower weakening?'

Robbing me of an answer, Bhiksham Dehi made his way through the ridges to somewhere unknown. He had been hitting at my stubbornness much more than required. The same mulishness which often thrust me uncontrollably towards everything forbidden.

Like any free animal, my obstinacy and I were alone in the forest now.

I lay on my back, stretched out on the rock. There was nobody to be stubborn with. The rock was in a relatively clear area, not crowded with trees. A meadow extended for a distance, filled with couch grass. A smattering of violet flowers. Wild bumblebees and honeybees buzzing with intoxicated delight.

The rock was like a majestic tusker . . . I could stretch myself comfortably . . . Catch the sight of the skies in the middle of the forest. I observed two eagles flying above. From time to time, one would go closer to the other and brush beaks, mesh wings.

A mongoose, which had half-circled the rock, stopped short on seeing me and, wondering what the strange animal was, raced away.

A chorus of wild crickets around me.

Some animal, meowing like a cat from the small hollow of a tree, was creating a din in the surroundings.

Abruptly, momentarily, all creatures fell into a meditation.

Total tranquillity.

Taking out my travel cohort, the binoculars, I turned to view the distant forest scenes. There were rosewood, butter tree and the giant crepe-myrtle growing luxuriously in the vicinity. Forest eagle-owls and red-whiskered bulbuls swung about in low creepers. A marauding group of wild monkeys were foraging, shaking the canopies. An unknown tree was doing a heaving dance, its leaves spread like an Australian pine.

Where was that smart aleck of a bird which made me lose my path yesterday?

Was its destiny to make me lose my way, to show me the way? If so, I shall not see it again. The bird's picture was in the camera. A picture which could catapult Freddie to fame!

But why was I taking the bird census or tabulating the charts? There was futility in defining nature in a few rows and columns.

These were just the fluctuations of the mind.

In what square was I going to categorize myself?

No idea!

It was through hunger that I was made aware of my own existence now. The limited calories in the rice gruel that I had consumed yesterday and the fruit had long been used up. The only way out in the middle of the forest was to wait for the mendicant's return.

The sun reached its peak.

When the rock started blazing, I made my way back to the den.

Filling my cupped hands with the dripping water, I assuaged my thirst. The great river was cool even in the afternoon.

When Bhiksham Dehi did not appear even when the noontide shifted, I thought of my own return.

On what belief should I continue here?

What was the guarantee that the man would come back?

If I started my downward climb, I would reach another refuge at least by evening. What if the mendicant did not return even after I waited for him?

Though Freddie the animal, caught in the wild, became jumpy, I decided not to get swayed by the mind's tempestuous thoughts.

The sun went down further. The shadows of the forest started falling on the earth.

Bhiksham Dehi was yet to return.

It was twilight. Bhiksham Dehi did not come.

My rumbling stomach was on fire, intensely desiring a fistful of cooked rice. The rice, obtained through begging, which I had vociferously turned down the day before, suddenly transformed into the greatest need of my life!

Night, surrounding me with its army, started displaying all its deadliness.

As hunger and the darkness started terrorizing me, I sat crouching in the corner of the den.

With the knowledge that no mendicant was going to arrive, crossing that formidable path, I lost grip over my own self.

Who am I?

All around was the exhaustive galaxy. In it, I, the only human. As the abject loneliness of the firstborn filled me, I remembered that even when I was solitary before, I had been fortified by the feeling of having people around. But now I was a manifestation of loneliness. Each animal in the forest was a loneliness.

The backpack carrying useless money was an extra burden to me. Impatient, I threw it to the side of the den.

In the world, there were only two faces of truth now.

Hunger and helplessness.

I could hear wild animals, as ravished as I, growling down below, having caught the human smell. They were attempting to scale the rocks. If some animal among them climbed the cliff, my helplessness would turn me into its dinner tonight.

A strong wind raged. I saw that the sky was overwhelmed with dark clouds.

Haum . . . Haum . . . Oum . . . Om . . .

The wind lashed the mountains and made a terrifying rumble.

As the beats of mourning inundated all my cells, I withdrew more and more into myself.

Today, I was just a wild animal, inside a cave, situated in the middle of a deep forest.

Just a wild animal.

12

PREPARATION

As the writing tapered off brusquely, like a vehicle stranded due to fuel drainage, I found myself bitterly disappointed.

The diary did not disclose anything about the events in the den afterwards.

One thing was for sure. Something had occurred in that disruptive and terrifying night that had led Freddie to transform into that wild man! An incident without parallel.

Maybe the mendicant had deliberately created adverse circumstances for Freddie Robert—pushing someone into the depths of helplessness and leading him to the discovery that he could overcome it. He might have survived snake bites after going through the experiences of the wild ant assaults. It must have been the resilience mustered during that night which had stimulated his disappearing act. It might have added a stream of oil into an undying fire within, causing it to blaze anew.

Yet, certain pieces of the puzzle were yet to be found.

Freddie could have become famous by presenting before the world a rare bird. Without attempting that, what was he searching for in the forests that was unavailable in civilized land? Or, what was he fleeing from, seeking refuge inside the forest?

Except from Freddie Robert himself, there was no hope of getting a comprehensive answer to that question. Else, one should reach that Bhiksham Dehi, who was waiting for a suitable begging bowl to fill with his alms.

I strongly felt that the mendicant had left after fulfilling his life's purpose. His existence there would have lost relevance after establishing a deserving successor in his place.

Nature has to maintain its own balance. Just like the earth stays balanced as a result of mutual interplay of many attracting and repelling forces, the truth might be that the forest needed a Bhiksham Dehi and now Freddie Robert had taken over that role. Even the breeze nudging its way into the room was an effort of nature to strike a balance.

Who knows whether the mendicant that Freddie Robert met had been a judge, a doctor or a scientist before the ascetic phase of his life? Those who had interacted with the man in the erstwhile days might have presumed that he had undergone a mental turnaround. Even if he was an error incarnate, that too might be part of nature's design.

Worm-eaten flowers, broken branches, one-legged crows . . . though human beings feel that these are aberrations, they are part of nature. There are certain callings which are to be shouldered by a single person. I have read somewhere that an undying idea shall wait for aeons for its flagbearer, despite being subject to crucifixion. When the world is embroiled in common rules and is tied up in knots, the flagbearer relishes the freedom of unravelling the bondages.

That is a distance which cannot be reached by those who proclaim themselves free. By calling the protagonist a 'crazy man', they unconsciously display their own imbecility.

Wasn't it that which my friends and I did to Freddie?

Contemplating that my thoughts were winding erratically over the forest paths, I felt astounded. How quickly had I started travelling through routes which had never been accessed till now, either in thought or reality! It would have been so convenient to denounce all those arguments as whoppers of idiocy! However, since Freddie's diary was in my hand, it was quite natural that its mental state transmitted itself to me.

I kept on aimlessly flicking through the pages with Freddie's descriptions, which had ended abruptly. After many empty pages, some notes in a sheet caught my attention. As if scribbling down a precious piece of advice, it ensued thus:

'It was due to his association with *Prakriti*, nature, that egoism and reasoning transpired in *Purusha*, the man. Due to that, he experienced sadness and joy over material objects, and the relative feeling of sin and goodness. It was Prakriti that turned the one bereft of any quality to the one filled with them. Surrendering wisdom, strength and freedom when one mingled with nature, all that remained was misery. It was not mingling but merging that was essential.'

It deepened my doubts that the words mingling and merging were underlined. Beneath it was the depiction of a yin-yang duality. A circle, half white and half dark. In the white half, dark spots; in the dark, white spots. When darkness flowed into white and vice versa, without any distinction between them, it became a full circle.

After few more sheets came another note:

'Like light passing through a crystal, through me, time has spread backwards and forwards. When I solidify myself, caught in the measures of time, I fall into the sad experiences of the past, present and future. Giving up solidity, when I acquire lightness, I flow from myself to everything. The wild dreams of the Neanderthal man, the dark tombs inside the pyramids, high speeds of the future vehicles, the settlements in the moon, all of it through me . . . The deep silence of the ocean in the mid-earth, the excruciating coldness of Antarctica . . . all are within myself.'

The Freddie Robert that we knew had never used mysterious words like these. I sat baffled like a school student staring at unfathomable scientific nomenclature.

This night at the guest house had robbed me of my sleep.

Four of the Pandavas were fast asleep, oblivious to their surroundings and fatigued by the journey. The Pandavas who had been interacting with me until recently—in which Indraprastha were they existing now? They must be experiencing as reality some lifetime which was beyond my understanding. If so, was the awakened me just a flicker of imagination in a sleep of mine?

I had a premonition after midnight, when I sat awake like Prakriti, even as Purusha slept.

Since Freddie Robert never maintained a diary regularly, why had he made all these notes and how come I, Meera, ended up perusing those near the forest in the night? Like the clasps in a thread of continuity . . . If so, there was a missing link to finally meld it all together.

In various stages of life, a similar intuition has come to my aid. Hence, I concluded that I had not accessed all the information in the diary. When my grandmother had passed away, relatively blind, at around seventy, we had discovered her diary, to our great surprise. No one could believe that she could write such a diary. But with an insight far sharper than those who had sight, grandmother had penned down the impending events in the family. Some mysterious facts which she had never revealed while alive. It flabbergasted us that those events did occur eventually! I had narrated that strange diary experience to Freddie and he had listened with keen interest. If that keenness had played a role in this diary, it meant that Freddie had something to say to someone.

To whom? What?

When the thought possessed me, I started examining the pages of the diary meticulously again. First, I quickly flipped through all the pages. Noticing nothing special, I turned each sheet very carefully. Though I repeated the exercise from left and then from the right, nothing of significance came to my notice.

I felt embarrassed by the failure of my sixth sense, which had foreshadowed a sudden discovery. Vexed at not getting what I was seeking, I forcefully dumped Freddie Robert's diary on the table. No, not dumped, I threw it on the table.

I had to sleep, since there was a trip planned the next day.

Suddenly, I felt a magnetic attraction towards the dark brown cover of the diary. Retrieving it, I fingered its outer cover, and a smooth, loose sheet fell out.

A transparent paper folded twice.

Seeing Freddie Robert's handwriting, greedily, I started lapping it up.

A letter which was written for someone, and remained unsent. Just a few sentences.

I had a yearning to wake up Mahesh or someone else or even all of them! There was no other way to clarify what was written in that letter. All four were in deep slumber. Stumbling on the serenity of their sleep, my urge to shake them awake became dormant.

Nothing about what would happen tomorrow was under our control. At least let those who sleep forget this world.

I thought to myself that I was a mother keeping watch over the sleep of her four children. A late revelation, that woman is nature and also the mother.

I checked the time. One hour of the new day had already passed. There was still no likelihood of any sleep for me.

Almost in continuity, another weird thought cropped up in my mind. I too must experience that solitary night which Freddie had spent in the forest.

One loses the equanimity to assess the consequences of one's actions when the time is imminent. When such a moment vanquished me, without waking up those lost in sleep, not even thinking that I was, after all, just a woman, I pushed open the door to the external dangers.

The sound of the latch bruised the silence of the night.

There was an assault of thick fog the moment the door opened. The medley of sounds emitted by the thousands of night prowlers fell upon my ears. Along with that, a loud growl, not very far, of a wild animal.

Somehow, I did not feel terrified on hearing that. I was listening to the sound of the forest without a thought about any looming attack.

Yes, the forest calls.

A primal call.

When I stood attuned to that call, I felt that Freddie Robert was in the vicinity.

To get to know him before anyone else, I put my foot forward into the outside world, where danger stealthily awaited.

13

NIGHT

When I woke up, the door of the guest house was wide open. Meera's cot was empty. The rest were in oblivious sleep.

Since Meera had been busy reading, we had not switched off the light in the room. Also, we didn't want her to feel anxious at spending a night in the company of four men. Yet, where had she gone, leaving the door open?

Though situated at the outer edges of the forest, the rest house was a problematic zone into which animals could wander.

Panicking at that thought, I went out through the open door, searching for Meera. When I switched the foyer light on, I saw Meera seated on the steps leading to the guest house, looking like an inanimate object. Unaware of even my presence, she was deep in communion with the darkness.

Leaning against the low wall, she seemed to have fallen asleep. But she hadn't.

Stepping closer, I called out gently, 'Meera.'

As if nothing extraordinary had occurred in the world, she asked, 'Well, Mahesh, couldn't you get any sleep?'

'Just woke up . . . Why are you sitting here in the darkness and the cold? Don't you know it is quite dangerous?'

'Danger,' Meera responded. 'Isn't Freddie living in this forest which has no roof or walls? Danger is also applicable to him, isn't it?'

'When someone selects something for himself, what can we do about it?'

'Mahesh, I feel now that there was something right in his choice! Do you think that someone like Freddie, always at the head of every venture, would do something crazy just like that?'

'He was very clear about what he wanted to do. I realized it when I went to him in the guise of the messenger. Then that last trip which we took together . . . Yes, I remember. That time, too, we had stayed in this guest house. Like you, Freddie stayed awake that night. Maybe he also had something haunting him. You know, he too stepped out of the room like this . . . And I went searching for him!'

'That is a broad hint that I might be lost in the forest tomorrow,' Meera smiled. 'Next time, there might be news that the nature researchers found a wild woman too!'

I was not in the frame of mind to relish that statement, said in jest. Meera sensed my obvious distaste.

'Sorry, Mahesh. Go ahead, tell me what happened that night!'

'I asked him why he wasn't sleeping. He replied that sleep was a relative experience. That one could sleep even with one's eyes open. Nature alone, he said, never slept. Apparently, he was studying nature's night. He also mentioned that man starts to become complete when he merges inch by inch with nature.'

My words intensified Meera's keenness to know more. 'And then? What did Freddie say after that?'

Flustered at Meera's unnatural enthusiasm, I muttered:

'He said woman was nature. That was why the union of man and woman became ecstatic. When man forgets himself in that trance, the universe vanishes. But while the merging with a woman was momentary, the return to nature would lead to infinite ecstasy. Since most of what he said was incomprehensible to me, I did not pay much attention.'

Meera's eyes widened. It was as if many elements which I had failed to understand were accessible to her. Perhaps a woman could easily sense that equation between nature and woman. A dread built up in me about Meera. I even wished that she wouldn't explore whatever Freddie had known. Knowledge can be very dangerous at times.

'Come inside, Meera. This cold isn't good for you.' More than the bitter cold, I was afraid of the heat being stoked inside her. We had to start for the deep forest early in the morning. It was a trek of almost 15 kilometres.

But she did not react to either my invitation or my anxiety. Instead, she asked, 'Mahesh, if we are going to search for Freddie, shouldn't we know what he truly was?'

'What's left to know?'

'Lots . . . lots. I studied his diary notes with the same studiousness as preparing for the examinations. There are certain missing links . . .'

'What?'

'You were the one to see Freddie last, right?'

'Yes.'

'I need to listen to the details. From you, directly.'

'It is already very late, Meera. Let us sleep now . . . we will catch up on our conversation tomorrow.'

'No, Mahesh. I insist on hearing it today. It is so very important in our investigation of Freddie's whereabouts.'

I had to succumb to the resolve in Meera's voice. Like
Freddie, Meera too never withdrew after setting out once. I
opened my memory book for her to peruse.

For us, it was another routine trip to the eponymous rock in
the forest: the Pullothippara. Once we crossed into the deeper
forests, a return would entail days. Barring Freddie, we were all
troubled by the forthcoming examinations and the classes we
were missing. Yet, we had set out for the journey to celebrate
Freddie's return after a brief stint of solitariness. Since it was
our last college trip, we had raucously revelled by indulging in
drinking, eating and singing.

Freddie involved himself to an extent that I had never
witnessed before. We were clueless that it was the extravagance
of someone who was relishing the singing and dancing which
would never come back to his life again. He hopped from rock
to rock, swam in the stream till he was weary, clambered up
every branch nearby. We viewed it merely as the boisterousness
of him becoming active in the Pandava gang again after a break.

Soon, when the celebrations became too intoxicating, we lay
in exhaustion on our backs on the rock and watched the skies.
The plan was to rest awhile and then start the return journey. I
had determined the time for the descent before closing my eyes.
I have an inner alarm clock; it was a mysterious trick which my
grandfather had taught me in my childhood. He told me that
if you determine the waking time, the *karnayakshi*, the female
spirit of hearing, would wake you up sharp at that time. There
was no need for any alarm! That was a recurrent phenomenon
in my life which never once went awry.

But before the female spirit's wake-up call, Freddie Robert
shook me awake. Warning me not to make any sound, he
pulled me by my hand deep into the secrecy of the forest. The
forest, dark even at mid-noon, seemed to have made Freddie

mad. 'Didn't I tell you that day about the first phase of nature? Here, this is it! There is no poisonous smoke here, no concrete, no treachery, no hypocrisy!'

In that moment, Freddie looked like a man returning home after spending a thousand years in a prison. Commenting that it was wrong to walk with footwear over pure nature, Freddie threw away his shoes and walked with naked feet on the wild path strewn with thorns and briars.

'And what for, this shirt?' Saying that, he unbuttoned his shirt and tossed it away.

He was infested with the vigour of a ship's captain who, after losing his way over the seas over many lunar months, had finally sighted the shore! While I stood bewildered at Freddie's tempestuous mood change—he was muttering 'I want to be one with nature's first phase'—he threw away all his clothes.

Had it occurred at the hostel, such an act would have been accepted as a pointless joke. How many times we had taken showers, stark naked, standing in a line on the third-floor terrace, next to the water tank! Never did we feel the need for clothes while swimming in a wild river when there was no one around. We have known one another, to the extent that no secrets even of the body existed among us. But this . . . now?

I asked him what that craziness was! His reply was it was one's own enslavement that made another seem crazy. He said with much feeling that he could not continue as an imposter, hiding a different being inside. Only when everything that kept a person from his own self was relinquished could one experience true nature. Holding my shirt, he blurted out that all the fastenings, including those of the buttonholes, were the first barrier. If we broke through those, we all would be free!

Maybe it happened accidentally in a moment when he lost his 'aham', his sense of self.

When my top button popped, harshly pushing Freddie aside, I retraced my steps to Pullothippara. I hardly cast a backwards glance at him. The surmise was that Freddie would eventually follow. In fact, I lost my way many times before returning to the rock where my friends were resting.

However, Freddie did not return . . .

What sort of a man am I? How many times have I regretted leaving Freddie, in that state of mind, behind in the forest? If I could not understand him, who else could?

Afterwards, though the four of us searched high and low, shouting ourselves hoarse, we couldn't find him. We lost him in the forest. We could find only his discarded clothes. But a piece of clothing thrown away is not a part of the human being at all. We left it there itself in the hope that he would come back and, clothing himself, return to us. We waited, but he never came searching for us. Had that news not reached us, we would have tried to forget him, thinking that he had ceased to exist.

I looked towards the forest that had absorbed Freddie. A forest that had swallowed darkness. There was uncertainty about the paths that we were supposed to tread at dawn. Tomorrow, we had to reach Freddie, overcoming the impenetrability of the forest with our mental fortitude.

'Meera, let's go inside.'

When I reached out to switch off the light in the veranda, Meera suddenly stopped me.

'Just a moment, Mahesh!'

As I looked at her apprehensively, Meera gazed at the pictures that graced the walls of the foyer. They were enlarged, laminated photographs of forest scenes, captured by an expert photographer.

I had not paid much attention to those pictures till then. One depicted the hair-shaking dance of the forest in a heavy storm. Beyond that, a group of deer staring at the camera, bewildered and ready to run; a white bearded monkey with its face cupped in its hand; elephants enjoying a river bath; a heron swooping down on a fish; a strange meditation of the great hornbill; and a pyramid of giant honeybees.

The most riveting were the scenes of an elephant pair mating, arranged in an orderly manner. In various pictures there were depictions of foreplay, erection and mating, which resembled a mountain merging with another. Although the pictures depicted animals, watching those pictures of sexual intercourse in Meera's presence was mortifying to me.

Meera, however, moved from picture to picture, observing with a rare intensity. Her mind was captivated by the ways of the forest. When she stood like a statue, I found myself growing acutely uncomfortable. I felt afraid that she had become part of those pictures, eagerly assimilating their essence.

When the forest scenes, inclusive of Meera, started throbbing in front of me, and eventually made me a part of that throbbing; I forgot that the dawn was incipient and that a full night's sleep had eluded me.

14

JOURNEY

We started off for the forest early in the morning. The purpose was to cover a large distance before the sun rose high. Only then would we be able to reach Pullothikkadu by afternoon, as was our aim. Everyone, including Meera, was apprehensive of the uncertain forest sojourn. The hope that the trip would take us to Freddie was the only stimulus.

When we began our journey, the fog was still thick. There was a cacophony of wild birds in the vicinity. A red mongoose stared at us meaningfully before disappearing into the leafy shrubs.

The forest is a fortress. At the frontiers, it looks as if the surroundings ensconcing you are protecting you from external attacks. There are profuse thorns, aggressive insects and gigantic trees acting as shields. Yet, someone forges a way through it, a keyhole to the heart of the forest. The width of the entrance reduces as one proceeds inwards, ultimately becoming a footpath. Occasionally, the diversions created by unknown people are noticeable. If we had stepped into one of those side-paths, we would have lost our way to Pullothippara—the eponymous boulder in the forest. Our first goal was to reach that rock where we had last been with Freddie.

On the frontiers of the forest, where thick creepers and huge trees abound, there are generally small animals and snakes. But there are predators in the deep forest, and hence the need for caution. Initially, we would always take along a Kani tribal, who knew the secrets of the forest.

The mentor of our former trips was a Kani tribal called Champathy, arranged by Maniyan. The brawny Champathy, who knew all the ups and downs of the forest and its very heartbeat, had a role beyond just that of a guide. Whether cooking food, carrying rice and other things or even handling animals in an emergency, his service was indispensable to us.

Champathy's relationship with the forest and his acuity in sensing the presence of animals were very famous. He often said that it was his early training that allowed him to identify an animal's whereabouts from miles away. His forebears had foraged in forests and hunted for their food. Appan Kani, his father, who used to guide hunters, had passed on the knowledge of the forests to him. Champathy's main organ was his nose, which could grasp the smell of any animal even from a distance. Watching the prowl marks on the wild paths, he would determine the species of the creature. Despite our best efforts, we could never make out the invisible claw marks that Champathy discerned. It was astounding how he could catch the 'sights' on the unclear paths, enmeshed with dried leaves and twigs, or even mud filled with pebbles.

Champathy could identify the particular animal by analysing the scattered, trodden gravel, crushed leaves, the leaning of the creepers and the grass, the leftovers of the leaves and so on. Examining the gnawed leaf he could determine the time that had elapsed after the animal had chewed it, and he would calculate the distance of the creature from the vicinity. His prediction that a bear or a leopard wandered at close proximity often rendered us fearful. Many a time, we escaped great disasters on the sheer force of his observations!

But we couldn't continue with that friendship for long. We got to know from Maniyan later that Champathy fell victim to a leopard while leading a team of hunters into the deep forest.

We did not accept Maniyan's offer of arranging a new Kani tribal as a guide in Champathy's place. By then, Freddie had grown intolerant of any external presence disturbing our tranquillity. We had become familiar enough with the forest to travel as a group. Freddie oddly believed in a wild truth about the forest: that 'the forest shall not betray'.

Once Freddie had decided something, there was no reason for us to doubt it. So we divided the materials needed for our trip and joined hands in carrying them. We typically camped near some stream. Kindling a fire using fallen logs, we cooked our food. When we slept, the roaring fire kept the animals at bay. At times, we spent our nights in tree houses in the heights. As part of our Nature Club visits, we had made some treehouses at different spots inside the forest.

This time, too, we decided to keep away from guides, ensuring that there was no breach of privacy. It wasn't a routine pleasure trip. Freddie might respond only if he met our group free of strangers.

One picture which became clear on studying the news report was that Freddie had appeared between two mountains, where there was the possibility of a dam construction. That was the place where the forest river gathered momentum. Freddie might be somewhere near the origin of the water.

We travelled carefully, observing every spot we crossed. Our search for Freddie's presence covered the creepers, trees and every asset of the forest. Even the pinnacle of the great trees did not escape our scan.

Initially, we chatted with one another. It could have been a way of reducing the tension or the eagerness at the start of our journey. But it did not continue for long. The undulations of the wild and serpentine creepers, which were ubiquitous, were draining us of our focus and energy. The earth, with its soil covered by fallen leaves, made us aware of uncertainties. Accompanying that was the fear of preying animals. An insecurity encompassed us while travelling, something unknown before.

We conveyed to Meera some forest rules which Champathy had taught us. If an elephant attacked, one had to run in a zig-zag pattern. The momentum, a product of mass and velocity, would make it difficult for the creature to change directions often. If the guest was a bear, clamber up a not-so-wide tree! The huge creature would not be able to sink its claws into a thin tree and climb up . . .

We did not disclose to her the secret that a female monkey with a red bottom was ready for mating.

Every step forward took us farther away from the normal world. The forest, apart from nature's magnificence, was turning into an experience penetrating our very essence. It insisted on demanding from us an awareness which we did not otherwise need in our living moments.

As soon as we entered the forest depths, we could hear the gurgling of the brook at a distance. When we reached it, keeping to the side of the stream, there were hours of climbing still left for us. That would lead us to Pullothippara.

The forest had almost hidden the secret that there was a fiery, blazing sun above it. Beneath the canopy that swallowed the sunlight, inhaling pure life-breath, we walked towards the river.

Meera was elated at sighting the stream amid the mysteriousness of the forest.

'How beautiful,' she called out, forgetting herself, 'how wicked of you all that you never brought me to this place before! Look, how lovely is that flowering tree leaning over the brook! The vastness of that giant tree standing beyond that! How clear the water happens to be . . . Not just Freddie, anyone would lust after this nature!'

One by one, we stepped into the stream. We sprinkled its water on our faces, trying to remove the fatigue of the journey. Wetting the hand, we cooled the nerve in the back neck.

There was no chance of a time-out here. We paused for a few moments, five or ten minutes at most, before walking on.

Through the fertile shores of the stream, crossing over furrows where fatigue abided, one had to move forward. The burden on the back made the journey tough. Snake-like roots which tripped one up, the sharp ends of leaves which flapped against the face, swamps swarming with insects . . .

'From every perspective, it seems as if nature is against us here. But that is not the truth. Nature is extremely agreeable towards us.'

That was Freddie's evaluation of the travel. He could see only 'oneness' in the various moods of the forest's elements.

Uttering an unusual sound, Meera attracted our attention.

'Hey, look!'

We concentrated our gazes at the spot where she pointed. Her focus was on the top of a lush, green tree.

'A stunning bird. Never seen anything like it before!'

True, an attractive bird which had never been a visitor during our multiple ornithological sojourns. A mélange of unique colours and a size relatively bigger than normal birds.

Maybe upon seeing the forest travellers, the pretty bird flew away from the tree and sought a perch in another one slightly farther away. Its cooing was a rather strange one. It rang out intermittently, like a life-song elevating one's mind to the heavens.

One could get a closer look using the binoculars.

'Oh, it is the same bird!' Meera interjected.

'Which bird?' Iyer asked.

'The bird which tempted Freddie Robert into the forest and made him reach Bhiksham Dehi! The Freddie Bird!'

We put her comment down to the natural effervescence of having experienced the forest's original beauty. But bolstered by the previous night's research work, she continued:

'This is a strange bird that no ornithologist has ever sighted. Whoever captures its photograph and sends it to the mainland can attain fame!'

'But we don't have a camera with us,' Muhammad Rafi sighed.

'No use even if we had one!'

'Hmm?'

'After sighting certain birds, you shall never return from the forest. You can publish the picture only on going back, right?'

'Can you please stop this chatter?' Sahadeva Iyer spoke fearfully. 'What if the time is inauspicious and what you say turns true?'

'So what? Are you insistent on going back, Iyer?' Meera parried in her natural provocative style.

By that time, the bird had started flying parallel to us, as if showing us the way. Singing melodiously at times, disappearing in intervals, flashing back into our sight afterwards . . .

'Listen, this bird is our first compass! Now we have to reach the sliced off part of a sharp cliff,' Meera said.

Brooding over the bird reduced the fatigue of that journey a bit. Could it be that by following this bird, which Meera had discovered, we would end up in Bhiksham Dehi's den?

However, disappointing us, the bird slipped away from our sights. Though we checked in all directions, it had vanished into some invisible hollow inside the forest. Even after a long while, not even its mesmerizing tweet could be heard.

Meera was the most depressed.

Still, we went ahead with our journey.

As time passed, the speed of our travel started reducing. By the time we reached Pullothippara, all of us were exhausted. Except for a herd of elephants relishing bamboo shoots nearby, we hadn't observed any other animals.

'Wow, beautiful! Really marvellous!' On reaching Pullothippara, Meera, overwhelmed with the physical loveliness of the forest, shouted in exhilaration.

Even we, who had a history of pilgrimage to that spot, became enthused by her adulation. Pullothippara and its precincts seemed more seductive than before.

The captivating gurgle of the cool flow circling the rock, and white pebbles, free of blemishes after having travelled through centuries, were visible all around. A holy chill, wherever one's foot touched. On the borders of that coolness was a veritable collection of small green plants. Occasionally, a camouflage of crickets, dressed in military attire.

Wild fish, uninhibitedly relishing the serene and clear waters of the stream, surrounded Meera, first in astoundment, then with inquisitiveness. Brushing against her fair calves, they started tickling her. Since their bodies were lustrous as glass, one almost saw their innards. Whenever Meera stooped to touch them, with great dexterity they slipped away. But there were kingfishers perched on tree stumps nearby, waiting to prey on the fish which tricked humans so easily. There were pied kingfishers, white-throated kingfishers and common kingfishers among those.

Like two equally powerful emperors, two stalwart mountains facing each other ruled the forest. And Pullothippara stood as a separate kingdom altogether, in the middle of the river flowing between those two crags.

It was certain that Pullothippara would be inundated if a dam connected the two mountains. Even then, declaring the inner secret of the continents, the mountains and the river would remain. The continents that are separated by the great oceans are connected underneath, and are, in reality, one landform. Hence, the earth has just one sea and one shore. Only birds and animals desist from dividing them with separate names.

On ascending Pullothippara, one could get a glimpse of the far-off river and of a sky trapped in the forest! Further on, the foliage became dense. Wild animals flourished therein.

'Meera, that day, it was here that Freddie . . .' Mahesh stopped halfway through.

'And here, we should start our search for Freddie.'

Heaving our backpacks onto the heft of the rock, we became free of encumbrances. One by one, we stepped into the silvery shimmer of the river.

Where, where was the presence of Freddie Robert, the critical brain of the Pandava gang?

'What if we shout loudly?' Muhammad Rafi asked.

Cupping his hands like a funnel, he shrieked into the ears of the forest.

'Freddie!'

A flock of strange birds took wing at that racket. The vicinity reverberated with the flapping of the wings. Meanwhile, we heard the sound of that bird, either from nearby or afar. It was as if the Freddie Bird was answering our call. A new vigour flowed through us, and imitating Muhammad Rafi's example, Sudhakaran started shouting.

'Freddie!'

Soon, Iyer, Meera and I joined in that invocation of Freddie, hailing his name as loud as we could. Our calls ricocheted off various craggy rocks. The forest started throbbing with the fullness of Freddie's name. It found a harmony in the recurrent cooing of the Freddie Bird.

How could Freddie Robert stay hidden, after the call penetrating the soul of the forest?

He had no option but to appear, either from some cave or from Bhiksham Dehi's den or from a treetop!

A sound rumbled from the skies. When we looked, a huge dark bear was foraging a beehive, clambering onto a tree branch leaning across the river. The tree was infested with lichen, which formed vitiligo-like spots on its trunk. As it tore open the hive, ignoring the panicked honeybees buzzing around it, the branch broke, toppling the bear and hive into the river.

The frantic bear, caught in the surge of water, reached Meera in a matter of seconds! In his frenetic attempt to escape from the rushing water, he lurched towards her with his sharp claws.

'The bear caught Meera!' Sahadeva Iyer yelled hoarsely and then sat down, shocked and drained.

15

LOSS

As the forest resounded with a cacophony of screams, Muhammad Rafi rushed towards the bear with a sturdy branch of a guava tree grasped in his hand. The unexpected fall, the frenzy of being caught in the water and the threatening shrieks must have combined to bemuse the bear. When it reached out, struggling against the onslaught of the water, it ended up getting its claws entangled in Meera's jacket.

While hysterically trying to run back to the shore, Meera felt the sharpness of the bear's claws through her jacket. With a weird cry, she pulled the jacket off and threw it backwards. When the jacket and the bear entangled in it went down in the forceful rush of water, feeling burdened with a weight heavier than what she had just discarded, Meera sat down exhausted on the rock. The bear, covered with the jacket, was tossed from rock to rock in the fall downwards.

We raced towards Meera, who had traversed from life to death, before returning back to life. Unable to believe what had transpired, she was panting. By that time, Sahadeva Iyer had recovered his composure to some degree.

For some time, all threads of communication lay broken between us. The five of us surrendered to a shared silence, incapable of fixing what lay shattered. At the start of our search for Freddie itself, here was the forest forbidding us, by providing an omen.

On recovering a bit of composure, it was Meera who started speaking first.

'I have read that while undertaking anything special, there is a likelihood of an initial obstruction.'

It was certain that Meera had more fortitude than the four of us.

'Some bit of good fortune still remains! Just imagine what would have happened if I hadn't decided to wear that jacket over my shirt and jeans. That bear would have hugged me with its sharp claws. We would have both gone hurtling down in a tight embrace. That did not happen! Just that I lost my expensive jacket!'

'If you want, I have a good one with me,' Sudhakaran intervened.

'Sure! I shall demand it when the bear comes to hug me the next time round!'

With the magical trick of transforming adversity into hilarity, Meera regained for the gang its lost vitality. After all, one ventured out on a forest trip only after anticipating the very worst.

'I feel very uncomfortable,' Sahadeva Iyer commented, 'as if we have made a false start!'

'Tut, tut, Iyer! Guess it was better for you to be in a forest full of kittens! If at all there exists one like that!'

Whatever bravado you exhibit with words, the forest is a gargantuan uncertainty. Meera's caution in ensuring that our spirits did not dwindle was appreciable indeed. To a certain extent, one could see in Meera a measure of the steadfastness of Freddie Robert, who used to say that both the universe and time paid obeisance to the brave.

'By the way, dear brothers, you have not bothered about the fact that I am freezing in my wet shirt here!'

We remembered the truth of the words only then. Meera needed a cover for changing her clothes. And it wasn't wise to let her be alone in any part of the forest.

'All of you, just turn your back towards me for a few minutes. In that time, I shall establish myself in my new clothes! God, hope no bear or tiger takes a peep in the interim!'

As Meera had suggested, we stood with our backs to her. In that overwhelming nature, where the forest itself became a cover, no one broke the rules to glance at Panchali until she changed her clothes.

'Good kids . . . At least for a brief period I could experience the freedom which Freddie knew. In nature's palpable presence, becoming a part of it, yes, it is a thrilling experience! Could it be that Freddie sent that bear to make me understand that?'

The forest took over her words. The long-limbed trees, standing with thousands of hands stretched towards the sky, listened eagerly. It spread, in the feral scents of the wild, where light never touched the ground. We were in the forest now. Dense forest. Every throb made us aware of an anxiety.

Until the shock caused by the bear whittled away, we continued to stay in that place. By that time, the purpose of our trip had been rekindled in our thoughts.

'We don't have time to fritter away whining over a bear's arrival! We should start searching for Freddie. Meanwhile,

Mahesh, can you please show me where you last parted from Freddie?'

'Yes, over there,' Mahesh said, pointing at a leaf-covered obfuscation. 'I only have a vague idea.'

'Doesn't matter. Shall we go to that place?'

'Definitely.'

We deviated from the topography of the stream and rocks to the inner forest. That area was covered with luxuriant green foliage. Pushing aside creepers laden with heavy leaves, we made our way, guessing the direction.

The small creatures in the wild scattered at the sound of dried leaves being crushed under our feet as we moved past red silk cotton and rosewood trees. There was a profusion of movement under the carpet of leaves. Huge spiders lay in wait, biding their time to trap us in their monstrous webs. We could see the mortal remains of the insects caught in their snares, fluttering in the wind. There was a sparrow's body among the victims.

Walking under a conjecture, we reached the spot where Freddie was lost.

There, a huge tree, its crown touching the sky, glared at us. It resembled a body builder flexing his muscles. Its magnificent arm-like branches were infested with parasitical creepers. Its foot was covered with many ancient termitaria. Could venomous serpents be inside? It was fearsome to watch.

'It was here, I remember!' Mahesh murmured.

On stumbling against something, Sudhakaran tapped it with his foot. It was Freddie Robert's forsaken footwear, covered with mud. Some curious wild creature had mauled it by biting through the straps. Slightly farther ahead, looking like a shed serpent skin, lay Freddie's rotting clothes. Like the physical body of the one who had attained enlightenment, the cloth casing was covered with termite hills.

For the Pandava fellowship, it was a heartbreaking sight, akin to digging up a body, long mingled with earth. It was similar to identifying someone, who had died much before his time, through a few pieces of evidence.

'Freddie . . .'

We were stunned when Sudhakaran shouted suddenly. He was someone who never raised his voice. Going against his habit, this was the highest pitch he had reached till now. The rest watched dumbstruck as the sound leapt unexpectedly from his throat. Sudhakaran seemed to be fully confident that Freddie would answer his call.

There was a rustling in the surrounding foliage then. Everything having life listened for a second to that call. The forest, including us, relapsed into a great silence soon. Crickets, birds, animals, all were silent. One second, bereft of a heartbeat, divided the time inside the forest into two. It started a new enunciation of time: before the silence, and after the silence.

We were stepping into the Shaka Era of searching.

Without lingering in the area for long, we returned to Pullothippara, our refuge in the forest. We were famished and exhausted. Since we hadn't rested on the journey, our bodies hurt. An impending search of the forest lay ahead, where our very lives would be held hostage. Before that, we had to eat some food. Then, as usual, a small nap in the lap of Pullothippara. Soon, our bodies would relinquish fatigue and become re-energized. The herb-scented breeze could absorb any type of exhaustion.

We entered Pullothippara, passing a tree that was constantly showering its petals on the river. Around that tree, which was glorious with red blossoms and hives full of honey, there was a carnival of butterflies and bees. A male butterfly, anxious to procreate, kept chasing its partner around the trees, like the heroes of old Malayalam movies. Meera watched interestedly as they swooped down on a bunch of flowers, one conjoined to another, to sip nectar. Two grebe water birds were competing with each other in the river. Periodically showing passion as well as competition, they were celebrating their mating season.

'How passionate is the forest!' Meera commented.

We took out the food packets from the knapsacks. One should never indulge in too much food at the start. Food should necessarily be modest, since we had no idea of how long we would stay, or whether a return was possible at all.

After having a light repast, we lay on our backs, next to one another, on Pullothippara. A forest is typically devoid of sky. Canopies are the forest's skies. The only sliver of sky visible was shining blue over Pullothippara. Our previous experience had been that life would touch elevated heights of a serene slumber, while experiencing the pleasing caress of a breeze, gazing at the slice of sky above.

It did not go wrong this time either.

But we did not know, as we closed our eyes in that mesmerizing ambience of the forest, that our waking would be in utter panic. When we got up, Sudhakaran was nowhere to be seen.

16

CAVE

I opened my eyes into the forest sky, at the sound of a call which broke my slumber.

'Irutte!'

Momentarily, in between awakening and sleep, I was ensnared. Did I really hear it or was it a figment of my imagination? Realizing that irrespective of whichever it may be, the call was smeared with Freddie's love, I hastily scrambled up in a seating position and gazed around. My friends, tired from the journey, hadn't been affected by that sound. If it was an experience restricted to me, it could be illusory too.

When there was a rustle in the nearby cluster of creepers, a thought-arrow rushed from me towards Freddie. I assumed he was there, having trudged from far away on hearing our shouts.

If my presumption was correct, Freddie was stark naked like a wild man, and consequently, reluctant to face the gang. Especially since Meera was accompanying us. Since I was the most eccentric among them all, he knew that I would understand him better than anybody else. Hence, though the yearning to call out 'Freddie' overwhelmed me, I suppressed it. What if he had something to share exclusively with me?

Without disturbing my sleeping friends, I walked towards the bunch of creepers.

Arjun trees and beach almonds grew lusciously there. Over them was draped *giloy*, which created the feeling of a green hillside. The way that amrit climber spread from tree to tree gave the impression of the continuous undulations of a mountain range. Two mountain squirrels were scurrying through the creeper, one chasing lustily after the other, leaping onto the branch of a black jamun tree. Their yellow tummies flashed in the air as they undertook that long jump.

After climbing down the rock, I crossed the arjun tree and moved towards the place where the leaves had swished. The invisible movement went farther away, as if measuring my steps.

I was bewildered. Was it Freddie or some solitary animal, separated from its flock?

Judging from the way it moved, it wasn't an animal.

Determined to find out, I flipped aside the obstructing creepers and moved to the mountainside. So long as the powerful pen torch gifted by Freddie and the skein of thread rolled into a ball were in the pocket of my jeans, I could go to any extent!

Could I be the first to step into this primeval place, untouched by any other human feet? As I edged forward, I detected the possibility of a cave opening by the side of the jutting rock. The movements that I sensed stopped at that cave opening.

My obsessive passion for darkness flared high at the sight of the cave. Could it be that Freddie Robert was living inside like a cave man? In that case, my presumption that I was the first man to step into that place was wrong.

The entrance to the cave was not very wide. One could manage to squeeze through. There were no signs of bestial stench or any other animals within. Fortifying my mind, I decided to enter. Even at the start of the journey, I had imagined finding Freddie Robert inside a cave and bringing him back to light. It was he who had filled my ears with the tales of the tribes hiding away in caves for years to escape from their foes. However, they lived together as a community. But Freddie had quit his group before taking up his dwelling.

As soon as I squeezed my way through, the space inside became capacious. It was a tunnel where I could stand comfortably. The walls were infested with clusters of roots and slimy wetness. The floor was slippery. There were streams of water originating from the rock.

When I moved forward a bit, the light inside the cave started dwindling. Retrieving my pen torch from the jeans' pocket, I shined its light into the pitch darkness ahead. Exhibiting all the signs of a cave that stretched beyond the reach of the torch's brightness, the light was hitting a faraway darkness. On battling innumerable small surfaces, light assumes a different character. Was Freddie Robert somewhere in that boundary separating darkness from light?

'Freddie . . .'

My hailing was not too loud. I could feel it meander into unknown places stridently, as an extended resonance, with intermingling echoes.

I stood awaiting a resounding reply to reach me, overwhelmed with my eagerness to meet Freddie. Then I walked forward. The expert in hide and seek would not appear so very easily.

If I wanted to showcase my love for darkness, all I had to do was to stand still without shining my torch. But no, I had to reach Freddie. He was the one who had introduced me to caves and taught me to listen to the infinite sound existing in a silent space.

Inside the cave, the throbbing of the 'letter of life' was discernible. The place was more alive than all the caves I had visited before. A stillness like the centre point of time's needles. Rather, time might be circling with respect to this motionless centre. But, where time was still, the universe should be still too. Could it be that Freddie had established himself in such a place?

If I wished to move further ahead, I had to affix some attachment with the external world. A compass to help me return. As I always did when entering an unfamiliar cave, I took out the ball of thread from my pocket . . . it would lead me on my onward journey. It was Freddie who had trained me in using the ball of thread.

I tied one end of the thread to a stone, and hung it over the branch of a tree. The 'pull' connecting me to the world outside was keenly felt in the thread. So long as that pull did not snap, I was safe inside any labyrinthine depths of the cave.

The strength of the pull was now the strength of my life.

Loosening the attachment which pulled me backwards, I started my forward journey. My footsteps were unspooling like thread, forward, forward . . .

If I had felt the presence of small creatures near the opening of the cave, now that too was absent. The quality and taste of the air changed. Meanwhile, I reached a juncture where the cave forked into two tunnels.

Two varying paths before me. They were insisting on a selection, and stretched separately in two directions.

Left, or right?

Where would each of the paths end?

It was then that I remembered the relics of the old palace situated in the valley. History texts give testimony that such tunnels were created as a final escape route during mutiny or war. My favourite subjects were history and archaeology. Hence, in the dynamic world of computer and Internet, I was always searching for the slow beat of history. Perhaps the insight that the tunnels were connected to the palace could be true. Or else, it could be nature's gift to the one seeking wisdom.

The calling of my mind made me take the right turn. It could be that I would travel through one path, only to meet the second and find myself at the same spot. The complete circle, where one sets off to find someone else, only to find oneself.

On that path, there were many rocks protruding into the cave. One drop of cool water skidded off a rock and fell on my forehead. I was about to trip over a round stone. As I frantically clutched the slippery wall of the cave, my fingers felt wet from the water dripping from the rock. From the stalactites which hung like slim pillars from the ceiling, lime water dripped steadily. Lime water is the favourite solution of chemistry lovers. When the clouds above mix with carbon dioxide and pour down, they make love with the limestones amid the rocks. Calcium bicarbonate, which is soluble in water, is the progeny of that affair. When it dissolves in the rushing waters and flows away, the rocks disintegrate, develop cracks and transmute into caves.

Nature must have taken many centuries to ready this cave to delight fans like me. But there was another chemical change which could turn fearsome. If the solution of calcium bicarbonate evaporates, the deadly carbon dioxide separates from it. In such places, which are devoid of life-giving air, death awaits. I had witnessed many skeletons of small creatures during my sojourns through the caves.

What would be the nature of this cave which was waiting for me?

Whatever that may be, a cave always reminds man of his limitations. Initially, each cave stirs an ineffable dread of death in one. The journey through the small intestines of a monstrous mountain terrorizes you with the fear of a devastation. Eventually, due to familiarity, one overcomes that feeling. For me, a cave was the most serene refuge.

For a little while, I leaned against the rock, becoming a part of it. Without the torchlight's beam, as I stood learning the darkness, listening to my own respiration, I heard another's breathing. Definitely, I was not the lone one to breathe in here. There was someone else who was inhaling the life-breath inside the cave.

Who? Who was it?

I flashed my torch light around, trying to discover the co-traveller. But I couldn't find anyone in the restricted ambit of the light. Yet, like the deep sigh of the huge mountain, there it was again.

Thrusting myself forward eagerly, I ended up at another crossroads.

In the brightness of the torch, I could see nature's severe stonework. The rocks were like souls that had been solidified alive. There was a deep silence everywhere.

But if one listened to silence, it would end up in a never-ending universe of sound. Silence was formed by the focusing of all sounds.

When many intersections arrived relentlessly, with no clue about the direction, I became anxious for the first time. The brightness of the pen torch was slowly reducing. The air was also growing thinner.

It was not wise to step forward any further.

'Freddie . . .'

I called one more time, only to end up utterly shocked.

The cave had swallowed my sound—like darkness gulping down light, death stemming the flow of life. I stood, staring bewildered at the cave which had shackled my call.

That, the nameless *that*, came and ensconced me.

Where was I?

The cave, like a spaceship, had accepted me and thrust me into an atmosphere that swallowed sound.

Here I was, in this capsule, like a robot that could survive without oxygen. The external world had become a faint memory that was light years away. Kuttanadu, the plentiful water reservoirs, my dark-skinned parents—all seemed to exist in a very distant past, beyond many births.

To make sure that the sound was dying, I tried to call Freddie once more. I tried to clap my hands to trigger sound. Both scared me by handing over an experience devoid of gravity.

This experience, which was beyond scientific interpretation, mocked my knowledge. Was the cave an emptiness lacking air?

I wished to return as fast as I could. There was no inclination in me to stand there as a man who did not breathe.

Since I had been travelling for long, I found myself exhausted. When I flashed my torch at my watch to check the time, I was stunned yet again. Having entered the cave at four in the afternoon, I had travelled till nine o'clock in the night.

I couldn't believe it.

To check whether the needles of time were lying, I closely examined the watch again. Its heart was beating in the normal rhythm. The seconds needle was also running fine.

Had the time machine run thrice as fast?

God, how many hours had I spent inside the cave? It would be night outside the cave too. I had been able to withstand everything only due to the technical finesse of the foreign torch in my hand.

The duration of five hours inside might be equivalent to fifty hours outside. It implied that my friends would be days apart from me. Alarmed after waiting for long, might they have returned?

When Freddie went missing, we had behaved similarly.

I decided instantly to retrace my steps. As I hurried, it dawned on me that my travel was a mesh of many sub-routes and twisted inner routes. Somewhere, the skein of thread had misled me. Night had thrown its infinite net over me.

Who was I now?

Away from the world, the mind and the body seemed to have separated in the silence, which spread into each of the living cells.

The dark-coloured one who lusted after darkness was merging into the infinite darkness.

I yearned for the tiniest sound. Leaving behind the great emptiness which swallowed sound, I had moved ahead. Now, the air certainly had the sensations of sound.

Feeling that I would be able to reclaim my courage by stamping my feet on the ground, I proceeded to do so. Not satisfied, I called again loudly: 'Freddie . . .'

The cave, which had gulped down the sound, spat out everything it had swallowed till then, and I found myself falling down, swayed by the powerful impact. I thought an earthquake had occurred.

In the unexpected fall, the torch flew out of my hands and rolled on the ground. In that flood of sound which made the cave quiver and shake, I lay in the darkness, unable to see anything.

As if the extension of a thunderbolt, the sound echoed along the inner tunnels of the cave and moved away. The only truth now was darkness.

It was not air that I was breathing, but darkness, darkness!

Lying where I was, I frantically searched around for the torch. My hands explored the centuries that the cave had lived through. There was neither dust nor moistness on the cave floor. Just rock. My trembling hands, which were caressing the crest and dip of rocks, stumbled across something strange.

My fingers sought out details of what it was.

They counted every rib.

A skull attached to the rib cage.

Arms stretched to the sides.

Legs that were folded.

With a recognition far more terrible than I have ever endured, I read out a skeleton in the darkness.

I was lying beside an ancient, decrepit skeleton. The only thing separating us was skin. The loving presence of a forebear, who had arrived centuries ahead of me, started becoming palpable. I recollected reading about the morphogenic field that exists in the universe, travelling through time.

Was it the forebear or myself?

Slowly, I got up.

Not searching for the torch, losing my sense of discretion, I stared into the darkness. Then I heard that breathing sound again. The inhalation and exhalation that made me feel that I wasn't alone. It started enrapturing me like a soft caress, in the gentle rhythm of a relaxed slumber. The great mountain's heart was beating slowly, devoid of any hurry. When it resonated with my breathing and my heartbeat, the last of the fear cells dropped away from me. Breathing alike, and throbbing alike, when the mountain, forebear and I became one, who was supposed to fear whom? Once fear leaves you, all that is left is simple bliss. It was as if all the scattered bits of ecstasy were coming together to focus on a central point. Every little joy I had sought, the blissful moments of solitude, were increasing my treasury, contributing simple interest and compound interest.

Slowly, the gentle rhythm faded away into nothingness. Then I heard it repeating in the opposite manner, gathering tempo and reaching a crescendo.

Takdam takidakida, takidakida, takidakida,
Takidam takidakida, takidakida, takidakida . . .

It made the rock that formed my roof and my floor throb, and made me vibrate too.

All the dualities were left far behind.

The silence that swathed the sounds, and the sounds that blasted from silence, were no more.

As the primal silence, the centre of all dualities, wrapped over me, leaving behind the motions of life, my body and soul recognized each other.

The ball of thread was exhausted.

I could not travel forward anymore. My mind, which was glued to the bliss of silence, did not wish to move backwards either. Again, as *that*, the nameless *that*, started encompassing me, in the mesmerizing ecstasy caused by the lightness of mind which relinquished dualities, pulling at the skein of thread, I broke away the connection that arose from the cave front.

17

DREAM

We awoke, with abject shock, to Sudhakaran's disappearance. As the search in the vicinity ensued, hordes of fears jointly invaded us.

In the forest where we had lost Freddie Robert, unable to find our 'darkness', we wandered senselessly, hailing him by name as loud as we could.

'Maybe he sneaked into some cave. After some time, he shall return,' Muhammad Rafi spoke.

Near the stream, the crags were like squares of natural rock stacked together. Monstrous slabs of rock, as if arrayed by ancient ghouls. Because their surfaces were vast and wide like cots, we could rest awhile by the stream. Sudhakaran had been resting on an isolated slab.

There were many dwarf waterfalls competing with one another, splashing on the wedges of rock. If one crossed the waterfalls and ventured deeper, there were many passageways. Could Sudhakaran have ventured inside one of those?

'Sudhakara!'

Although we created a havoc which reverberated in the forest, there was no response. Our calls intermingled and ricocheted off the stone slabs, and the bats dozing away in the wild jamun trees frantically took wing.

'Bat . . .' Sahadeva Iyer gazed up with distaste, 'that is the harbinger of ill luck.'

The rest of us ignored that uncomfortable observation. What we needed was a bird spouting positivity. Like the one which had arrived to guide us on our forest sojourn.

But no 'good-luck birds' appeared. Only the grotesque mammals flew around. They are strange birds which consume more than their body weight in food. After circling around for a while, at an opportune time, they returned to hang upside down on the jamun tree. They were sparring with one another, clutching and shoving.

The forest had usurped another of our beloved friends. Where were we supposed to search for him? The belief that he was somewhere in the proximity prevented us from delving into the deep forest.

Muhammad Rafi climbed onto the highest point of the rock and relentlessly called out for Sudhakaran.

In the journey meant to seek Freddie, how quickly had Sudhakaran evolved into our immediate crisis! We travelled for some time, moving upwards and downwards the riverine path.

'First Freddie, now Sudhakaran . . . if it continues like this?' Meera's voice broke.

Sudhakaran's vanishing act had added to her trauma after she had escaped from the attack of a bear by sheer life-force, exhausting her. Sudhakaran's bag, now an extra weight, seemed to be staring at us. The excruciating sight caused anguish to Muhammad Rafi too.

'Unjustified,' Rafi muttered. 'This journey was totally needless. What is the guarantee now that we shall not end up losing ourselves?'

It was as if the theme of a horror movie that we had seen together had suddenly started playing in the surroundings. A story where the members of a research team in the forest mysteriously disappear one by one. In real life, we were being forced to face that hackneyed, inauspicious motif.

Sudhakaran was the most peaceful among the Pandava fellowship. Someone who kept to himself in the deepest conversation or the biggest crowd. There was no history of Sudhakaran raising his voice, or expressing any insistence regarding any single object, anytime ever. His voice would never go beyond a particular decibel level. If you depicted his life, it was a straight-line graph, devoid of any ups and downs. And then, after bending and breaking that straight line, where had he suddenly disappeared?

The shadows were falling in the forest.

Now, colours dimming, the darkness would spread. The creatures of the night would start prowling for food and mates. We had to find a night refuge fast.

It was the first night in the forest without Freddie Robert, who had contributed the most to the gang's total courage. The rest of our fortitude had drained away, having lost Sudhakaran. We did not have the strength of mind to spend the night by the river, huddling around a fire.

The fatigue of long travel, the mental anguish of having lost Sudhakaran, all of it had pushed our minds into barrenness.

'No more.' Meera sat down exhausted on the wild path covered with dried leaves, putting down her travel burden.

The woman who had started the forest trip declaring a war on any gridlock, was shorn of strength. In the harsh show of might between hope and reality, we were losing our inner resilience, like her.

We did not have the resources to survive the forest beyond two or three days at a stretch. Bread, biscuits, a few packets of dates, some rice and spices. Our existence was dependent on those; an unending forest stay was not our goal.

At that moment, with a shudder, we remembered Freddie. How had he survived the unknown forest with not even the reserves for a single meal? During our journey, we had sighted only rare fruit trees. Could the forest have kept aside, in some place unseen by us, means for life's survival?

Time was ticking on.

Without receiving any clue about the whereabouts of either Freddie or Sudhakaran, our first day in the forest was coming to an end.

While suffering over the lost ones, the existing ones should not be forgotten. It was necessary to find a place to rest at night.

As part of our Nature Club activities, we had constructed treehouses at various locations in the forest. While we thought of staying in one of those, perhaps due to the overall anxiety and lack of focus, we did not succeed in finding any. In the search, however, we strayed into a fearsome spot.

There were scores of snake skeletons scattered in that particular location. The remains of the snakes, lying solitary, some entwined with others, a few heaped together . . . it reminded one of gruesome pogroms. Sahadeva Iyer uttered, 'Ah!' and turned his face away hastily. Unable to take a step further, we decided to withdraw from that place.

There was a profuse growth of plants here which killed the serpents by weakening them. If any snake crawled past unknowingly, it would get enervated. Unable to slither away, caught in a frenzy, it would end up losing its life in the vicinity. The remnants of such hapless creatures, which had lost their lives over time, were strewn around. Once Freddie had observed that there were places inside the forest where there were mounds of human skeletons. We hadn't given that remark much credence, dismissing it as a fib which the normally truthful Freddie happened to utter. Our doubt was about skeletons of humans appearing inside an uninhabited forest. The reply had been a grin. When it was time to leave the body, animals and birds seek out hideaways. The same was the case with human beings who had merged completely with nature. They couldn't be discerned by anyone, and no one knew where they had blended in.

On seeing the snake skeletons, we were forced to think that Freddie hadn't lied while making that appalling observation. 'The unknown was deeper than the known': ruminating thus, we gave up our goal of reaching a treehouse , and retraced our steps.

It was then that we glimpsed a beautiful snake, its body imprinted with a royal ring pattern, crawling exhaustedly nearby. Despite its best efforts, it couldn't move an inch. Possibly, death was close. Though it was a venomous snake, it was heartrending to watch it struggle for life. Poor thing, let it escape if it could; Mahesh used a stick to scoop it up and throw it away. Yet, it did not fall far from the toxic plant, and slithered on the ground again. After trying many times in vain, announcing that the snake was doomed to die, Mahesh gave up the attempt.

It was then that Meera spoke, astounding everybody: 'Just hold on before taking a final call!'

Without an iota of fear or revulsion, she bent to pick up the weary snake in her hands, and walking a long distance, placed it down carefully. The serpent gazed at her gratefully through its tiny eyes.

'If it regains its life-force, perhaps the snake clan shall shower us with blessings!' Sahadeva Iyer cracked a joke. It seemed as if he was peeved with Meera's sudden fraternity with animals.

'Us? Well, I rather doubt if you, Iyer, are a part of that "us". Be careful when you trundle along. There could be more snakes around!'

Hearing Meera's pert response, Iyer's eyes filled with fear.

Wild animals were observing us from hither and thither. Sambar deer were the first to step into the vicinity, rather hesitantly. After drinking water at the stream, and expressing their aversion to us, they raced back into the forest. A gang of civet cats came out from the tree hollows, ready for hunting. We were haunted by the terror that a tiger or leopard would soon appear.

'We have to ascend the highest rock around. Animals shall not cross the waterfalls and reach that,' Sahadeva Iyer suggested, trembling.

Like a lot of tales, it was just another belief. On our forest trips with Freddie, we had camped there during the night. We would make a circle of fire with kindling, and sleep safely in that enclosure.

Carefully, we started climbing the rock. There was only one way to while away a forest night. Hold on tightly to an ineffable sanctuary. Or else, trust that the forest shall never betray, as Freddie believed. The one who was not treacherous was indeed a true friend. So the only way was to transform into a true friend of the forest.

With our bundles, we reached the highest summit of the rock. All of us had been exhausted to the point of death in just a day. Far away from our quotidian life, it felt as if someone else was living out some other life.

'Not that this place is very secure. That there are four of us is the only comforting factor!' Iyer said.

'What about Freddie and Sudhakaran then?' Meera's voice was tearful. Losing her reserves of strength, she sobbed openly.

'Meera, cheer up.' Mahesh patted her on the shoulder.

Though we were famished, nobody ate anything. The food in the bags remained unshared.

As if pouring from the skies, a prattling group of blue parrots swept down to roost on the huge tree by the riverside. The king of the trees was readying itself to meditate for a long time, after having shed most of its leaves.

Both, the fear of animals and the anguish over the lost ones, prevented us from sleeping. Usually, we took turns to watch over the others on such trips. Tonight, breaking from routine, we were all staying awake.

Not very far, animal grunts could be heard. The forest was coming to life.

At some point, Meera slipped into a slumber, totally weary. Hardly had she dozed off when she shrieked 'Sudhakara!' and leapt up.

Muhammad Rafi flickered the gas lighter on.

Meera was drenched in perspiration. Her body was extraordinarily warm. In the forest night, there was no medicine, no treatment, no hospital.

Stretching her arm towards the lighter, Meera checked the time. Nine o'clock!

There were many hours left before dawn.

'Tomorrow we should find that den,' Meera said, 'the den where Freddie ended up. In my dream, I saw Sudhakaran there too!'

Our hearts were sundered, and the remains dispersed into the dark recesses of the forest.

'However, there was something else,' Meera muttered.

'What?' we enquired eagerly.

'I saw something else there. Something that encompassed in one second, the saga of years! What was it . . . what was it?'

Anxiously, Meera started mulling over whatever it was that had slipped beyond her reach, when she was supposed to remember it without fail.

18

LEITMOTIF

The dream had slipped away but seemed to yield in just another moment. On coming closer, it again evaded my grasp. Despite all my endeavours, I couldn't gauge what I had seen. Whenever I tried to recall the vision to share it with my friends, it kept away from me. As I affirmed to my mind that I wouldn't disclose it to anyone, and the purpose was to convince myself, both memory and loss became equidistant. Finally, I had to pledge that I wouldn't confess it to anybody even if I remembered that fleeting reverie in its entirety. Then, miraculously, all the snippets that had been sliced away from the dream were resurrected. Complete, in all visual perfection.

The first sight was the river that flowed, dividing the forest. It rushed, like the flow of infinite time. As if formed from water, a woman took shape, and swimming past the crystal distance, she approached the man waiting on the riverbank. When she emerged from the water cover, her body dripped many rivulets, like the great mountain sending forth rivers. The streams stumbled over the undulations of her physique, and seeping inside her, partook much from her, and the water following soon after, filled up the crevices.

When she walked out of the water, a river sprouted from her forehead, crossed the tip of her nose, fell down and flowed through the narrow channel between her full breasts. Two tributaries flowed from the left and right shoulders, respectively, and passing under the curve of each breast, all three flows merged in her navel. From there, the Triveni Sangam, the combination of the three rivers, moved towards the *Jaghana moolam*, the intersection of her behind, and then mixing again with the main river, immersed in the *Aadi moolam*, the origin of life in her womb.

Observing how all the rivers originated from her and ended with her, the man sat on the shore. The man looked at the woman, and the woman looked at the man. Her thick tresses, hanging past her behind, gave her a wild beauty. She was now a wild palm tree, with roots deeply entrenched in the earth. He was entranced at the sight of the wild palm with its flowing hair. The eyelashes, which were moist and meshed, the rosiness of her cheeks, the crimson of her lips, all were enough to trounce him. She was enticing the man with everything she possessed. Slowly, rising up from the water that covered her hips, the woman approached the man on the shore.

From the state of she being water, and he being shore, she came so close that water transformed into shore. Wherever her foot touched, the earth became wet and confessed the story of mutual immersion.

The woman had the radiance of a newly born soul. And the man was just a shape that had lost its name. Her eyes took in his primeval nature. His hair and beard were long. The wild growth of chest hair grew profusely and coalesced at his navel. Without any inhibition, the woman gazed at the sign of his malehood. And he returned the look. Fundamentally there existed only one sign. The sign of subtraction. The symbol of addition was just a delusion formed by criss-crossing two signs of subtraction. Just an extrapolation from the fundamental symbol.

The thought that the addendum of the addition sign had been waiting for a long time for the fundamental deletion sign in the forest stoked a frenzy of love inside her.

'Shall we take a walk through the forest?' Ensconcing his hand inside both of hers, the woman queried.

It was the month of Shravan in the forest. In Shravan, even those meeting for the very first time felt a lifetime bond. They would feel the familiarity of having stood together in the forest darkness. They walked under the sacred figs in fruit, brushed past the mahoganies, and meandered beneath the mahwa trees. Tiger families strolled by, readying for a drink of water. Majestic tigers looked evocatively at them. Tigresses walked by with their cubs next to them. The little tiger cubs curiously snuggled against the humans, sniffing happily.

The woman picked up an adorable tiger cub and planted a kiss on its face. The man scratched its back. His fingers touched the woman's breast, tickling her provocatively. That prompted her to hug the tiger cub closer.

The woman freed the cub and let it run towards its mother, who had been patiently waiting nearby.

The man was not surprised by the subservient attitude of the wild animals. He had come to realize that when animals and humans met at a point of sharing nature's bliss equally, animals became peaceful. The forest was no longer indeterminate; instead, a most natural cordiality. It was Eden, where no one quarrelled with one another. Had he not recognized that, he would have fallen prey to a wild animal a long time ago.

The couple travelled alongside a herd of elephants which were breaking bamboo shoots for their food. Tossing their heads and frolicking, elephant calves brushed affectionately against them. A little farther ahead, a recalcitrant tusker raised its trunk at seeing them. A king cobra, with a 'V' on its hood, slithered past their feet devotedly.

'I feel tired,' the woman spoke after a while. 'Can we get something to eat?'

The man looked around.

Seeing the honeycomb on a tree branch, he climbed the tree with the vigour of a wild man. Enjoying the naked man's ascent, she stood under the tree. The man did not crush wild cumin leaves and slather them on his body to prevent bee bites. No honeybee would dare touch him. When he reached their honeycomb, the honeybees saw him as just another one of them. Near the tiger, he was a tiger, and near a tree, a tree. For him, the body was just the protuberance of an existence that was deeply rooted in the past.

Until he reached her side with honey brimming in a leaf-cup, the woman waited on a rock. He had brought sweet fruits along with honey for her repast.

She bit into one fruit.

He ate from the same.

Then she took a bite again.

Afterwards, he.

Repeating that rhythm, after a few times, the fruit disappeared, unknowing who it was that had tasted it last.

The man dripped the honey through the small hole at the leaf-cone bottom for her to sip. When her tastebuds filled with pure sweetness, she swelled up with fullness. She made him taste the honey too, the cone held close to his lips. The threads of honey flowed from his lower lips, through the beard, his chest, and showered on his nakedness. As she used her lips to lick the trace of honey, the man stood electrified with passion.

The heat of the honey was enough to provoke both their bodies. The woman sprinkled what remained of the honey over the man, and he did the same.

Greedy insects swarmed around the two bodies doused in honey, as they stood glued against each other. When they tasted the manna on each other's body, the insects joined the melee, completing that ritual. They were standing under two gigantic trees whose branches had meshed with one another. The tree was not a mere tree. The human was not a mere human. Rather, the human was the tree itself. The body was just the protuberance of an existence rooted in earth.

Memories have no origin or end.

Obliviousness has both.

Where oblivion begins, memory dies. It was at that juncture when his memory faded that he woke up almost in a trance, and an adolescent's embarrassment caught hold of him. He started brooding about his nakedness.

His discomfiture caused the woman to be mortified too. When a shyness, hitherto absent, takes root, it becomes a bevy of shyness. She too transformed into an adolescent. When the man gazed at her body with passionate curiosity, she tried in vain to hide the thrusting breasts. He relished the sight to the utmost—that of her struggling to hide her nakedness with her insufficient hands.

The woman's lips were reddened and trembling. The man started melting in the heat of his passion on looking at them. When the anxiety of being exposed to each other's nakedness left them, first she and then he, started smiling.

Braiding wild creepers together, she made a garland for him, making him her man. Putting the same garland around her neck, he made her his woman. Then, entwining his hands around her neck, he embraced her in his arm-garland. The creepers spread on his body, and stretched taut like nerves. When the southern wind started blowing wildly, the woman suffocated in his manly strength.

In a long kiss which began during the origin of the universe and would not end even in the final floods, he detached her from duality. Even to the extent of making the woman forget her primeval pride that *she made him a man*, he made her a part of oneness. Like an atom forgetting itself in the infinite essence.

A man who reaches his prime, crossing his adolescence, is like a tumultuous hurricane. He is sky-high in his stately manliness. In that stature, it was forbidden for the woman to control him. Like a handmaid, she started caressing him from his feet to the locks of his head. Shedding all her adolescent inhibitions, like a Devadasi who had mastered the art of making love, the woman started provoking his manhood using every organ of hers. She used all her sense organs of action and knowledge, lips, tongue, limbs, in taking him to the pinnacle of ecstasy. The fact that he was aroused made her passionate. In the summits of great mountains, in the furious rushing flow of magnificent rivers, in the eye of the cyclone, the whirl of the seven seas, in the molten lava of the centre of the earth, in the bone-chilling coldness of space, in all of these she reached him. In the moment of their meeting, sparks of fire and thunder flowed through him. When the last thread separating them broke in orgasmic ecstasy, they transformed into the forest, into the sea, into the sky, into infinity, became nothing.

The man's sperm fell into the woman's womb and became the seed of the universe.

After sharing his sperm, the man had become empty. Without leaving behind even a memory, carnality left him totally. Like an infant sleeping in the woman's lap, he lay serenely.

How innocent, like a baby, he was now! A crystalline purity bereft of any fluctuation of passion. It hardly took a moment for the woman's motherhood to stir. Caressing his tresses, she fortified his tranquillity. In that resting state, as his eyes became drowsier, he hugged her with his childlike hands. Feeling his tender touch, her breasts swelled with milk. She wished to breastfeed him.

Bending to his infant slumber, she kissed his forehead. In his drowsiness, he called, 'Amma'. That call was enough to melt her.

She wished to make him sleep. For the naughty child who would sleep only on listening to the stories of merging, she had kept aside a few stories.

'If you want to hear a story, close your eyes.'

'I have shut my eyes.'

'What has the child seen with his eyes tightly shut?'

'Forest, mountain, river.'

'Look intensely.'

'I can see the sky. Fire too!'

Though he hailed his mother from the atmosphere of radiance, she did not reply. His calling continued, and morphed into that of a toddler who could not speak words.

'Mm . . . mma!'

His age started decreasing from three to two, then to one, and even lower. He suckled at her breasts as a six-month-old infant. Shook his tiny limbs as a one-month-old baby. He gave a toothless grin. Then, crossing beyond the moment of birth, he became the foetus curled up in her womb. There, he was branched off into twenty-three pairs of chromosomes, bearing the inherent essence. Going further backwards, he became his own sperm that was ejaculated inside the woman, and turned into a seed. Retrieving what he had offered, and offering himself what he had retrieved, he blended and merged in one another.

By then, my dream opened the window to the night in the forest, and roughly shoved me into life's conundrums. While sleeping in a strange forest was a luxury in itself, I had lived through a dream-like experience in all its intensity. But I had promised my mind that I would never reveal it to anyone else. When you cannot share a dream with anyone or even speak about it, the best name for it is 'life'. In the company of three friends, how quickly I had become isolated!

19

LETTER

Though we searched throughout the next day, we couldn't find the mountain with its crown sliced in the middle, the den that had accepted Freddie, or the monk who was the link between all of them. We ended up circumambulating a very tough terrain, muddled by a mountaintop far away. Such crags were common all around. If all of them were to be examined, it would involve more than a day for each. We had neither the resources nor the time for that venture.

It was a formidable forest with ferocious animals. Considering that we had escaped the attack of a striped tiger due to sheer luck, we did not dare to explore another mountain. That great royal of the forest, having finished a sumptuous feast, was lazily resting when we passed by a short distance away, totally unaware of him. The tiger gazed at us as if we were another animal of the forest. Since he was not hungry, following the law of the jungle, he let us go scot-free, like any other animal.

Afterwards, in every inch of the forest, throughout that search, we were terrified in the expectation of a hungry tiger nearby. Sahadeva Iyer, rather timid by inclination, insisted on going home with the fortuitously granted second life.

However, even in the span of one day, we had become acquainted with the gigantic trees gloating with braggadocio, and the wild animals jostling with one another. In our search for Sudhakaran and Freddie, we examined every aspect of the rain forest. From the canopies holding their heads high to the clinging creepers which depended on the dim sunshine to the covering of small plants—everything came under our observation. We had no clue where to search for both of them—at the top, in the middle or lower down.

Thus, when we touched the forest through all its inscrutabilities, Meera raised an opinion. 'The forest has a certain truthfulness to it. On becoming closer, it seems to be turning in our favour . . .'

'That was exactly what Freddie said. The forest shall never let go of the one who comes seeking willingly,' Mahesh acquiesced.

'At least the animals of this forest shall not attack anybody,' Meera responded.

'Hmm. Why?'

'They might have been transformed into peaceful creatures by now.'

Everybody seemed to be in the mood to endure the apparent paradoxes of the forest. But where was Freddie? Where was Sudhakaran? If the forests never let go of anyone, where had they received refuge?

It would not be possible for us to continue with our search beyond another day.

'Will we find them before that?' Sahadeva Iyer became fraught with worry. 'Or are we fated to abandon them both in the forest?'

Since Iyer had found a treehouse during the day's trip, our problem of a night stay was solved. The treehouse was on top of a tree of extraordinary girth. A centurion, very ancient indeed. Five human beings with locked hands would be needed to circumscribe its span. In its essence hid many door frames for innumerable houses, many Jesus Christs for countless chapels, and many crosses for them to bear. When we edged closer, a primeval humming seemed to ensue from it.

There was a thick rope dangling from the great body of the tree, to take us to the treehouse. There were knots on the rope for climbing: our stepping stones from death to life.

Like those carrying the yoke, with the knapsacks on our back, each started the rope climb. Mahesh reached the treehouse first.

Meera followed.

Though we were doubtful about her prowess with the rope exercise, she clambered to the top, throwing all our doubts to the wind.

Unwilling to abandon Sudhakaran's orphaned bundle in the forest, Mahesh descended again to lug it up. We watched miserably from the treehouse as it lay like a corpse on his shoulders.

It was apposite that we had set up many such treehouses in different parts of the forest. Freddie Robert's long-sightedness!

We would usually travel with the Kani tribals, who were experts in crafting treehouses. They would easily climb up even the most monstrous trees. By hacking the bamboos that grew by the riverside, they made sturdy treehouses. Freddie tied colourful ribbons to the trees to indicate the paths to the treehouses. Except a few that had been mauled by naughty wild creatures, the rest were still fluttering about. It could be that such treehouses were giving refuge to Freddie Robert in the deep forest. Could it be that he had been dedicated to

building such tree-havens since he had already planned his
forest exile?

Having been secured against the dangers of the world
below, our thoughts travelled again to Sudhakaran and Freddie.
Sudhakaran's bag lay pathetically in a corner of the treehouse,
like an orphaned dead body awaiting a post-mortem.

When the forest darkened, everything living and non-
living acquired a stillness. The birds roosted, tucking their
wings in. Only the mobile phones of the wild crickets kept
chattering sporadically. Their 'ranges' were intact even in the
remotest of forests!

Muhammad Rafi kindled the gas lighter.

Since we could not afford to keep it flaring, he turned it off
soon enough.

The four of us huddled against one another in the small
treehouse. Meera was seated between us.

There wasn't space enough for anyone to stretch their limbs
due to the crowd. We could sit sleeplessly, sharing our woes,
that was all.

When the tenebrous darkness descended, bloodthirsty
night moths manoeuvred an attack on us. Insects, many
times in size compared to the mosquitoes back home. When
a light was shown, they shilly-shallied into the distance. The
moment the light went out, they continued their guerrilla
warfare. However, the flicker of light couldn't be sustained
till morning.

After spending most of the night fighting off the marauding
insects, a strong wind started blowing, and the treehouse
swayed ominously. When the thunder crackled, creating a
terrible sound in the forest, birds fled away in the darkness,
screeching and wailing. Below, there were movements of
terrified animals running for their lives. A wind, having begged

around in a thousand villages, had entered the forest with its restless mind.

The centuries-old tree where we were seated started heaving and shaking in the eye of the storm. The treehouse seemed to be on the verge of collapsing.

Why was it that everything had turned against us today? Oppositions, not known till now . . . As if the forest was yearning to tell us something.

The storm's *tandav* continued unabated. If there was a heavy downpour, our situation would be precarious.

Meanwhile, a bird roosting nearby started making inauspicious sounds.

'*Kuthhichudum . . . kuthhichudum . . .*'

'The mottled wood owl that supposedly wails on sighting Yama, the Lord of Death!'

Hardly had Mahesh spoken when Sahadeva Iyer insisted fearfully, 'I want to go back, tomorrow morning itself.'

He was trembling, as if he had lost his life at the cliff of depression.

'Then you better start right now,' Mahesh snapped, his voice bristling with rage. 'How profusely you praised Freddie! Fees, mess . . . such adulations! And when facing a quandary, you simply care only about yourself!'

'Just because someone lost his marbles, should others follow suit? Now we have lost Sudhakaran too!'

'Let it get lost—your life and mine! Now that we have set out, I am determined to get a result!'

Frustration was raising its head among us. Yet Meera was traversing far away from the arrow tips of words. When the momentary wrangle subsided, she called out: 'Mahesh!'

'Yes, Meera?'

'Now I can see clearly . . .'

'And what is it that you see clearly in this pitch darkness?'

Since we were huddling, our body temperatures mixed with one another's and reached the same level of heat. Above the haven of the tree, rain passed, not deigning to fall.

'Freddie must have spent many nights in this treehouse,' Meera said.

'How do you know that?'

'I was not just skimming through his diary notes. Those were visceral experiences for me. Maybe he had written them down for me! Like an indicator to point out his immense yearning to merge with nature in this forest . . . Besides that, I found an unsent letter he had written for someone inside his diary.'

'A letter?'

Along with Mahesh, the rest of us were astounded too. Though we couldn't see each other's faces, the expressions were obvious.

'It was tucked away inside the brown cover.'

'What . . . what was written in it, Meera?'

'It was a letter written to a woman. A woman named Kamala.'

Kamala!

That name caused us all a great shock.

'Well, do you know anything about this Kamala?'

Each of us intensely pined to leave Meera's question unheeded. Like a chieftain who was on the verge of defeat in a war, losing control over our words, each of us collapsed into his own self. Meera had nailed each of us on the crosses hidden in that tree.

At that moment, Meera opened Sudhakaran's bag and, retrieving the promised jacket, started donning it. Realizing that we would be facing a morphed form that was Sudhakaran outside and Meera inside, we sat in the darkness like statues carved from the very darkness.

He, Sudhakaran, had promised Meera his jacket in the place of the one the bear had taken with it and that had been fulfilled like a prophecy.

If so, what else was going to be fulfilled in this forest?

20

KAMALA

The name which we wished to keep away from had arisen from Meera's tongue, catching up with us. Her question had thrown us into the depths of a confusion that had no answer. Never had we thought that the woman called Kamala, unknown to Meera, would reach even a remote forest. The forest was mysterious, and what happened inside it, was more incredible.

What answer could we give Meera?

Beyond the fact that we had a feisty Panchali as namesake in our Pandava gang, Meera was also an ideal friend to us. It had achieved the zenith of a flawless male-female friendship. More than anyone, it was Freddie Robert who was determined that the bond would stay unstained forever.

But beyond the world of Panchali-Pandava inclusive of Meera, we had a parallel world of male fraternity. After college hours, Meera couldn't be with us. We had celebrated the hostel as an independent nation. Freddie had even rented out a house for indulging in liberties which went further, and locked it up. To open at will, to use as desired . . .

At the inner beckoning, we camped in that rented house, drank ourselves senseless, and watched pornographic movies. Our lecturer, Xavier Francis, owned a movie theatre nearby. We watched second shows when sizzling hot movies, which burnt up the veins, played there. It was Xavier sir himself who brought news to the college of the heat quotient of the flick. In the plant engineering class, while elucidating about nuclear reactors, using secret codes, he would throw open the potential of the new movie. The style of conversation, sticking to the dignity of a teacher, concealed a mutual understanding. He said nothing, and we noticed nothing. But there would be a great rush for the second show that night.

While we watched the movies once, there were lust-crazed fellows like Sahadeva Iyer who achieved hat-tricks and beyond. That was a different world. Their beds were made softer by the 'little books' purchased cheaply by the wayside. When the 'call' came, they exchanged their book stacks. The general theme in all were sleazy tales of sex, with enticing, salacious titles like 'The Delightful Annamma', 'Lusty Nights' and the ilk. Except Iyer, not a single one among us, especially Freddie, had any inclination towards such tales, which were sordidly stunted in both language and imagination. Freddie would accompany us to the sexual possibilities of the second shows only on our insistence.

The woman, Kamala, had been the discovery of one such night when we visited the theatre after a drinking binge. Freddie Robert, who was reeling under the drink, must have felt attracted to some factors in the woman waiting for customers with a randy laugh. The ingredients for sexual arousal in the porn movie which we had watched that night might have been another reason.

Kamala was much older than us. Though not very pretty, she had an uncommon charm about her. She too was pleased with the rich man's offspring who sent her back with handfuls of cash, unlike her usual night partners. When their get-togethers happened more than once, Freddie had laughingly spoken about how Kamala had developed an unwarranted obsession with him.

'Do you know what that slut told me today?'

'What?'

'That I should give her the gift of a son! A good progeny, with the engineer's beauty and brains!'

'What greed, considering the hussy's old age!' we had chortled with mocking laughter.

But the woman called Kamala was an enigma that we couldn't fathom. Someone who carried with her something different from the other prostitutes on earth. She fantasized about how blessed she would be in accepting the seed carrying the legacy of engineering. It could also be that such an ordinary woman, hitherto used to relationships only with substandard men, had become overwhelmed by the stature and dignity of Freddie Robert. Eventually, she stopped meeting him. She was not be seen in the usual places again. We sensed that Freddie was affected rather seriously by that wilful absence. We remembered a monologue of his during that time.

'The greatest weakness of a man is the lack of control over his own body. It is the body, indeed the body, that should be overcome first and finally.'

Not only did he divulge that, he started ignoring his body in all manners afterwards.

With the passage of time, we forgot Kamala. Freddie must have forgotten her too, or so we assumed.

Never did Freddie indulge in anything dissolute again. He kept away from all forms of intoxication. Through discoveries of his own, he turned more and more solitary. Even studies became something unwanted. Freddie punished his body harshly by not coming to the college mess in time, depriving himself of food. He started searching for a truth beyond the body, by returning to nature.

Freddie said that a man who had lost attachment to the body will not be afraid of anything. He was truly experiencing it. That was how he garnered the courage to travel to the forest, all by himself. The meeting with Bhiksham Dehi stoked his passion for merging with the primeval purity.

We narrated to Meera the tales of our sinful habits with much embarrassment. It was fortunate that the darkness hid our visages. Yet, we were apprehensive that she would loathe us and abandon us due to our exposed hypocrisies. How could she trust the three unworthy men who sat brushing against her in the middle of the forest?

But Meera did not respond as we feared.

'You were wrong,' Meera spoke. 'None of you knew how that *poor* Kamala betrayed Freddie! Avoiding birth control measures, unknown to Freddie, she had already taken over a part of Freddie's life. One should presume that it was the impact of that shocking news which made Freddie undergo a total transformation and made him retreat into himself. He was unable to handle the trauma that his own life was germinating inside a womb as old as the one in which he had lain! All his sensual desires left him. His search for understanding how nature became nature must have started then. That must have been the meaning of his jotting in his diary that "*It was not mingling but merging that was desirable*". For Freddie, a return to nature was both atonement and union. The woman called Kamala, ignored by everybody, never met Freddie again. She went away, not wanting to burden Freddie with her life. We do not know where she went or whether she gave birth to Freddie's child.'

Our bodies froze; the bones, flesh and nerves undifferentiated. We were dumbstruck and unable to utter a word for a long time. The secret which Meera had uncaged inside the forest had shattered us completely.

We were late in recognizing our Freddie in all his originality, something made possible only through Meera. It was the forest that revealed him. Yes, to understand Freddie, it was imperative to have a forest, embodying the pure presence of nature.

Our eyes hurt with the yearning to see him that very moment. He was ours, and not an atom's distance should separate us from him. We wanted him unconditionally, regardless of all that had happened.

'Yes, it shall happen tomorrow,' Meera murmured in the dark.

'What?'

'We shall find Freddie.'

Meera's voice was firm as that of a prophetess. We could see the word glistening, and the sparks rising uproariously into the sky in that darkness. The vision, which should have travelled from the eyes outward, had pierced the inside through a reverse journey. All sights were within.

Unexpectedly, from the tree where we sat, a bird took flight, cooing loudly.

'Look, the Freddie Bird,' Meera cried out, unable to control her joy, 'it was so close to us all the time!'

A situation in which even those sceptical about coincidences would be left without argument . . .

To think that the bird had been with us all the while, so near, so near.

21

DISCERNMENT

As we sat in the nest-like treehouse in that great tree of the forest, it struck us that the bowerbirds which fascinated Freddie would have a nest of the same size. We were four such bowerbirds too. Tiny, hapless, blind fledglings whose eyes were yet to open. While the forest showcased each of its weapons, the only option was to endure it inside the bird's nest. Though we were together, it felt as if each was stranded in his or her own remote forest.

Throughout the night, sounds could be heard in the vicinity of the treehouse. As if reminding us that we were not alone in the heights of the trees, some dynamic movements, here and there. Though we tried to shine a torch in the direction of the Freddie Bird's flapping wings, the light failed to penetrate the thick canopy. To somehow quicken the night to morning, we wrestled with its seemingly unending elasticity. When it finally happened, the dawn turned out to be totally bleak.

When the light exposed the great tree fully, it sunk in that we hadn't been alone the previous night. There was a horde of monkeys in the neighbouring branches. They were watching with astonishment the intruders who had taken over their home. They were probably wondering which species the encroachers belonged to! We returned the curious gaze.

'Are they likely to harm us?' asked Sahadeva Iyer, who found a scope for doubt in everything. But the simians looked amiable, without any antagonistic attitude. We searched for a branch without monkeys, expecting the presence of the Freddie Bird who had shown up the night before, but the effort was in vain. Going away when we needed it, and edging closer when we did not, what was it trying to tell us?

Filtered through the luxuriant foliage, threads of light squirmed their way down to caress us. Drawing enthusiasm from it, we decided to start our descent.

When Sahadeva Iyer started to climb down, the monkey troops, as if provoked suddenly, started a hubbub, chattering and jumping from branch to branch. We were apprehensive that they might unleash an unexpected onslaught. If they pounced on us as a group, we certainly wouldn't be able to fight them off, seated in that treehouse.

The monkeys, however, were not aggressive towards us.

'They are warning us!' Meera spoke.

'What warning?'

'Look carefully, maybe a tiger or a leopard is hiding nearby!'

Hearing her words, we observed the world below with alacrity. Behind the thicket, underneath the creepers, was there a hidden maneater? Such animals could sniff human blood from afar.

The perspective from the sky did not yield any results. But without being sure, we couldn't use the rope either. While we sat befuddled, Muhammad Rafi pointed downwards, yelling.

'Look, over there!'

The looks which followed his finger's direction focused on a single point. There was a serpent resembling Shiva's own snake, a *Rudra Naag*, coiled around like a knot at the bottom of the rope. It was extraordinary in its size. When the threads of sunlight fell on it, the speckles on its body glittered like slivers of glass.

Looking at the simian ancestors reacting strongly, Meera said: 'Did you see the way the forest works? Each protects the other!'

Baby monkeys, sensing danger, clutched the bellies of their mothers. The faces, as innocent as human babies', were gazing downwards at the threat below.

'It is slithering upwards!' Sahadeva Iyer spoke, terrified as if the snake was at arm's length.

Mahesh and Muhammad Rafi undertook a joint effort to shake the upper part of the rope heavily, to banish the snake. But it stayed firm, unwilling to be detached from the 'rope of his desire'. In the world of illusions, where a rope was often misunderstood as a snake, here was the unique sight of the entanglement between a snake and a rope! Meera seemed to be relishing that intermingling between truth and deception a lot.

'Look, another snake winding around the snake dangling from the great tree!' she quipped.

'Oh, a tender poetic heart at play amid utter danger!' Sahadeva Iyer mocked openly.

'Instead of whining, watch and enjoy, Iyer! You get to see this only in a forest.'

In the long duel fought between snake and humans, the human beings were pitiably defeated. Whether it had accepted how the hood of human pride was bowed, or it was bored with the rope-trick, the serpent uncoiled itself from the rope and glided away into the forest.

Yet, we dared to touch the earth only after ruling out danger, after having spent a long time above. The monkeys too scrambled onto branches and dispersed into the wilderness. They too were travelling in a group, like us.

As soon as he reached the ground, Muhammad Rafi caught hold of a thick piece of wood.

'Might come in handy.'

Meera conjured another simile to describe the weapon.

'As if a snake has solidified . . .'

We moved towards the rivulet. Our exploration had become small sojourns which started and ended at the stream. A few trees had fallen into the river and were decaying, as if incapacitated in the past. A cormorant, its wings spread, was perched on one of the fallen trees, resembling a newly fashioned cross.

Conducting our morning ablutions in hidden places, washing our faces in the cool river water, we became active again.

For us, it was the third day in the forest. Also, the last.

Each of us was feeling utterly empty with the arduousness of the journey and the lack of sleep. Unless something hot was consumed, the spines would refuse to stand erect.

We made a makeshift rock stove. Making a bonfire with some gathered twigs, we huddled near it. Meera made some milk-less coffee, with a kettle of water. In the forest, an ounce of that liquid was akin to nectar.

While sipping the warm drink, Meera said: 'How original! No cooking range, no gas cylinder. No electric wires hanging like cobwebs under the sky. The rumbling of vehicles is kilometres away. There, we rush helter-skelter, and over here the world moves at a slow pace, not wanting anything. The sun and the moon are the lightbulbs, the wind is the fan, the stream provides the waterline . . . I have started feeling something too.'

'What?' Mahesh asked.

'Don't you remember the three fundamental units we studied in physics, Mahesh? Metre, kilogram, second: the units used for measuring length, mass and time. The rest are all derived units, jerry-rigged versions of these.'

'So what?'

'Mahesh, life also has just three fundamental units! Hunger, lust, excretion. If these three are fulfilled, a human being becomes satisfied. The rest are all jerry-rigged versions of these, all artificial! That is why the forest becomes a refuge for those seeking a return to the fundamentals.'

'But lust . . . how can that be satisfied in the forest?' Muhammad Rafi queried.

'Did you think lust meant just sex? It is a feeling of union. Won't you get that a thousandfold while merging with the universal body than just mingling with a single body? Freddie was discovering the immense potential for that in the forest.'

'Sure, there is also the possibility of choosing whether one's death happens by getting mauled by a tiger or a leopard!' Sahadeva Iyer snapped at Meera's words.

Meera, usually given to quick retorts, pretended not to have heard that sarcastic response. She was immersed in some other contemplation.

'We should take a dip. Else we will be fatigued,' Mahesh interjected, trying to change the topic.

'Yes,' Meera agreed, 'but before that, let us stroll by the riverside. Should search the dens near the riverbank.'

Deciding to follow that suggestion, we started the search of the third day by hailing 'Freddie' and 'Sudhakara', as we had done the previous days. Not just the birds and the animals, but the trees too must have learnt by heart the human names reverberating incessantly in the forest. How was the forest, comprising all of those, going to react to the names today?

As the river flowed, marble-like white pebbles could be seen strewn all around. There wouldn't be any slush in the waters when there were trees nearby. Hence both the water and the pebbles were crystalline pure. In the flow, the tiny resistance offered by the pebbles was creating alphabets of water . . . When the life-giving water touched the feet, there was a direct communication with the heart. It was an experience affirming that the foot was equal to, if not superior to, the heart.

After meandering through more such experiences, we sat down on another side of the boulder. The structure of the rock was different over here. It looked like perfectly heated limestones, full of calcium.

While the others sat with heads bowed, depressed by the lack of results and unsure of the plan ahead, Meera was still standing in the stream. Stooping, she picked up a sparkling pebble and put it on her palm.

We were in the spot where the research group had discovered the forest dweller. The focus point of all our searches had been this spot. If a forest dweller called Freddie was alive, he had definitely heard us. But the fact that he chose not to return to us—did it imply that we would never get Freddie or Sudhakaran back? Or, had our minds lost their strengths of transmission, unable to reach them?

'What did this meaningless journey give us? Only loss.' Mahesh sounded weary.

'Wish we hadn't seen that news item! At least we wouldn't have lost Sudhakaran': Muhammad Rafi was almost whimpering.

'I told you so right in the beginning! We should never have come,' Sahadeva Iyer seized the opportunity to protest.

'Has Sudhakaran met Freddie? I feel so . . . Suppose, if he too realized whatever Freddie did? . . . What then?' Mahesh wondered aloud.

But Meera was not responding to anything. After making a prophecy of discovering Freddie Robert today, in what silence was she steeped? She was twirling the crystalline pebble in her palm, as if she had no part in the ongoing discussion. Iyer seemed to be peeved by her indifference.

'Think of the grand announcements you made yesterday! What about that bragging . . . that you shall discover Freddie today?' Sahadeva Iyer taunted.

'Today . . .' Meera murmured, covering the pebble with both her hands, 'the day is not over yet, Iyer! So much of it still remains. If Freddie pushed aside the wild creepers and appeared right now, wouldn't my prediction turn true?'

We shuddered on hearing those cryptic words. Though we had been relentlessly searching for him, if Freddie appeared before us suddenly, we would definitely be dumbfounded.

As if we were not prepared for such a moment, we looked around warily. When the anxiety spread that Freddie might appear out of the blue, making Meera's words come true, she continued to keenly examine the pebble in her palm. Through the transparent surface of the pebble, the lines of Meera's palm were visible, including her heartline and lifeline.

'Here, I have taken the universe in my palm. How transparent it is! It has become purified by the flow of water over the centuries, and hence the limpidness and transparency.'

Hearing Meera mumble to herself, our looks fixed on her.

'This is the first phase of nature. A transparency devoid of covering or treachery. If so, Freddie is very near this transparency!'

Sahadeva Iyer cast a penetrating glance at the one who was going erratic in her speech. Meera was handling the pebble as if it were alive.

'Now she has started blabbering in daytime, after making prophecies in the night! Probably got infected by Freddie's disease . . .'

We felt that Iyer should not have been that corrosive in his speech. Meera, however, remained passive.

'Iyer, why should it be a disease? Can't it be an awakening?'

'I can see it only as a disease.'

'If it was a disease, all Freddie's generous help to you was a part of that disease. Paying your fees, the mess dues, calculator, books . . .'

We watched Iyer retreating into his inferiority, and turning silent. Still, we did not take offence with Meera.

'I think Freddie's child must have been born.' Meera shocked us yet again. 'By birth, one is in the first phase of nature. The thread around the child's waist is the first tie with the artificial world. With that, losing his purity, he starts viewing nature as separate.'

'What . . . what has happened to you today, Meera?' Mahesh asked agitatedly.

'What is the goal of our journey, Mahesh?' Meera asked him a question instead. 'To discover Freddie, right? But do our eyes have the ability to see him, though he might be as close to us as that bird in the tree? Tell me, when he called you to go along in that last forest journey, why couldn't you do it, Mahesh?'

When Mahesh hung his head like a sinner, Meera continued: 'You were unable to understand what he recognized. But now

I can see clearly how a man, Purusha, becomes complete through nature, Prakriti. One should merge with the other, and vanish through that union. Through that final nakedness, Freddie could achieve that. Yes, woman is Prakriti. Does nature have the tendency to hide anything, anywhere? One needs a fig leaf to hide the shame, in that moment of separation from nature. If what prevents one finally from experiencing nature is that which hides her from her own self, why should anyone want it?'

Meera was pulling us inside a magnetic circle. The profuse sunlight was making the river water sparkle more brightly. After seeing the green of the forest for days on end, our sights too had turned green. Green, green, green all over.

Then, through the green, we watched Meera freeing herself of the barriers to nature. When she renounced her clothes one by one uninhibitedly, our Panchali, whom we had never seen completely, became known to us for the first time.

Her nakedness did not cause any provocation in us. Manifesting as an untainted sculpture in the longitude and latitude of time, when she stepped into the crystal-clear water, we saw in her the spreading trees, mountains and the infinite sky.

The wild invitation of nature, free of all covers, took hold of us momentarily. Unable to refuse that call, following Meera, each of us freed ourselves from our casings, and stepped into the eternal momentum of pure and transparent water.

Scan QR code to access the
Penguin Random House India website